RETURN

(THE INVASION CHRONICLES -- BOOK 4)

MORGAN RICE

CHAPTER ONE

For the longest time in the darkness that surrounded him, Kevin was convinced that he had died. It felt right somehow. Everyone had told him that he didn't have long to live anyway, and then there had been the spacecraft drifting in the emptiness, the air running out little by little. After all that, *shouldn't* this be the end of things?

"Kevin," Chloe's voice called from somewhere in the space beyond that blackness. "Open your eyes."

"G'way. I'm dead," Kevin mumbled, because a part of him just wanted to go back to sleep. It wanted to drift off and relax, letting the blackness overwhelm everything. He was so comfortable that… He winced as something pinched his arm. "Ow!"

His eyes shot open to reveal a room that definitely wasn't the ship they'd been floating helplessly in. This wasn't a stolen Hive craft, where they were slowly dying after being winged by an Ilari craft and the wreckage of their world. This space was larger than that had been, and it looked almost like…

"This is a hospital," Kevin guessed. He knew what hospitals looked like by now. He'd spent so much time in hospitals, and labs, and other places that it was impossible *not* to recognize it for what it was, even though it only looked like a hospital in an alien way, with none of the devices looking like the ones he was used to.

"You're awake then," Chloe said, from the spot where she stood beside Kevin's bed. She looked faintly satisfied with her efforts to wake him up, smiling to herself in a way that suggested that she would be more than happy to do it again.

"That hurt," Kevin complained, and then a thought came to him. "Are *you* hurt? Are you okay?"

"I'm fine," Chloe assured him, sounding serious now. "They patched up the worst bruises when they brought us here."

Kevin looked her over anyway, wanting to be sure, and worried that she might be trying to hide how hurt she really was. Someone had given her a kind of silvery uniform to wear in place of her usual clothes, which looked a little like the silvery scales of a fish, reflecting the light in different ways as she moved. As Kevin looked down he saw that he was wearing the same thing.

"How about you?" Chloe asked with obvious concern. "Are you hurt?"

"No," Kevin said. "I don't think so."

He definitely didn't feel any worse than he usually did, or at least, than he usually had before the Hive had chosen to make him one of them. He had pain running through his body, and dizziness threatening to rise up inside him when he moved too fast, but Kevin knew those feelings. They were so familiar that they were almost like old friends by this point. He couldn't feel any of the sharper pains of anything broken over the top of it.

Chloe came forward and hugged him tight. "I'm so glad you're safe."

Kevin held onto her, even though he didn't feel like he deserved it right then. It was his fault that it had come to this. If it hadn't been for him, Chloe wouldn't have been stuck in a cell, undergoing experiments. She wouldn't have the strange, alive-looking thing bonded to her arm, tight as a second skin, its bony, insect-like surface seeming completely out of place against the smoothness of her skin.

It felt so good that she was safe that for a moment or two, Kevin didn't even think about who was missing.

"Where's Ro?" he asked, looking around for the former member of the Hive. "Is he—"

"Good, you're awake," a new voice said. Kevin turned to where a door had opened to reveal a blue-skinned Ilari woman in a dark uniform with military insignia. Kevin recognized General s'Lara from the com-cast he'd made trying to trick her and the rest of her kind. Just the thought of it made him sure that this must all be some horrible dream.

"General, *you* saved us?" Kevin said. "But I… I tried to trick you." That wasn't the worst part of it though. "I… I played a part in blowing up your world."

Guilt flashed through him at the thought of all he had done, while he saw the general's expression flicker to one of anger.

"You also helped to warn us," she said. "That gets you some consideration from us, and… well, we don't want to abandon people in need. *We* are not like the Hive."

"That's…" Kevin didn't have the words. "Thank you."

"Don't thank me yet," General s'Lara said. She glanced up, and she seemed to listen to something only she could hear. "My AI tells me that the others are ready to decide what to do with you. You *and* that so-called 'Purest' you brought with you. Follow me, please."

"Kevin's still weak," Chloe argued. "He needs rest."

"He can rest all he wants once the trial is done. Now come with me." The general was clearly used to having her orders obeyed, already walking without waiting to see if they would do it.

Kevin looked over at Chloe, who shrugged. They knew that neither one of them truly had a choice. Hurrying to keep up, they followed the general out of the hospital room, into a set of twisting corridors whose walls had shimmering images that gave them the illusion of broad, open spaces. Here and there, Kevin and Chloe passed windows that held a view out into open space.

"We're on a ship, aren't we?" Kevin guessed. It didn't feel the same as the Hive's ships. This one didn't have the perfect stability of gravity drives, but it was still definitely a ship of some kind.

"This is the flagship of the escape fleet," General s'Lara said. "My AI is integrated with it."

"So every inch of this place is… you?" Chloe asked.

"I guess you could say that," the general replied. "My AI will connect to the others for your trial."

"Like the Hive?" Kevin asked, and instantly knew from the general's expression that it was the wrong thing to say.

"We are *nothing* like the Hive," General s'Lara said, in a sharp tone. "They force themselves upon the worlds they destroy, upon the people they make a part of them, upon each other. The misery, the *choices*, of others mean nothing to them. We join with our AIs, but we still choose what we will do, and we seek no conquest. We sat behind shields because we did not wish to slaughter others, even though it cost us *worlds*."

Kevin could feel another wave of guilt rising up in him at that. He'd been the one to help bring down those shields and make their planet vulnerable to what came next. He'd been the one to help the Hive destroy their world, and take his. To his surprise, though, Chloe was more direct.

"You could have fought them and you didn't?" she said. "You hid away from them when you could have *stopped* them?"

"Chloe—" Kevin began, but it seemed that Chloe wasn't done.

"No, Kevin," she said. "If she's saying that they could have done more, that they could have beaten them before they got to Earth, then they could have spared all of us this. They could have saved us."

"We couldn't even save ourselves," General s'Lara said, looking mournful now. "We don't have the tools to stop the Hive. We can kill them, we have the technology to beat their ships, and they just keep coming." She seemed to listen to something again. "No, I know. Anyway, we're here."

She gestured to a set of doors. Kevin and Chloe stepped through, into a large space filled with people. As with the corridors, images spread over the walls, but these seemed more abstract, and Kevin could see the patterns in them. Somehow he knew that this was the AIs communicating with one another.

Ro stood on a blank circle of floor raised above the rest of it. Kevin hurried over to the alien, wanting to make sure he was all right, while Chloe was even faster, throwing her arms around him. The people there stared at them. Kevin could see so many of them, both Ilari and other aliens who had taken refuge among them, that it was hard to pick out individual faces. Even so, he knew that they were staring at the three of them without looking away, trying to make up their minds.

"Ro, are you all right?" he asked. His friend didn't look hurt, but even so, he seemed shaken.

"I don't know," the alien admitted. "I am feeling so many emotions. Guilt, and fear, and… how do people *cope*?"

Kevin put a hand on the alien's shoulder. Chloe put an arm around him.

"We do," Chloe promised him. "And we keep doing it."

"These three were salvaged from a floating ship," General s'Lara said, obviously addressing the assembly. "You can see that one of them is one of the Hive's 'Purest.' Of the others, one is the boy who helped to let them into our world, while the last has been changed into one of their creations."

Kevin hated hearing him and his friends described like that. The worst part, though, was that he couldn't deny what they were saying about him.

"We are on our way to another outpost," General s'Lara said. "The ship tells me that our fleet is being stalked, and so we must decide what we are to do with our new guests. Can we risk having them aboard? Are we in more danger by having them here? Are they all that they appear? Are there any who wish to speak regarding the first of them? The girl?"

There was a swirl of images and letters on the walls as the AIs communicated with one another. If he concentrated, Kevin felt as though he could get the gist of their conversations, the signals that made them up transformed for him through the same talent that had let him translate all of their other signals…

…not guilty in all of this…

…a victim, not a foe…

…the device on her arm though…

Two individuals stood up.

"It has been decided that I will speak for her," a man said. "It seems obvious to us that she was a captive of the Hive, their victim, and not one of them. We should give her safety as one seeking refuge."

A woman stood up. "It has been decided that I will speak against," she said. "Although we have sympathy for her plight, we do not know what the aliens have done to her. The item on her arm could be a risk, because the Hive do not design anything *safe*. We should contain her, or destroy her, for the safety of others."

General s'Lara nodded to Chloe. "Do you have anything to say?"

"What do you want me to say?" Chloe snapped back. Kevin could see that she was close to losing her temper now, and that probably had a lot to do with how scared she was.

"Then I will say it," the general said. "We are not a people who kill because there *might* be a threat. Chloe here is as much one of us as any of the others who have come to the Ilari in search of help. I believe that she should be welcome among us, and perhaps in time, we will be able to reverse what was done to her. Do any others wish to speak? No? Then we will talk of the others."

Kevin felt the general's gaze rest on him, then on Ro.

"The arguments around the others are more complex," she said. "One warned us of the attack, and helped us, but was also the one who brought down our shields. The other is one of the Hive's Purest, and so our foe. I know that our people are peaceful, but I find it hard to feel anything but anger when faced with this."

Kevin looked at the walls, and now the writing buzzed around less like fireflies and more like angry bees. The arguments seemed far more complex, and his talent for translation only gave him snippets of it this time, so that it was impossible to follow along completely.

...where does responsibility begin...

...where does it end...

...If he is one of them, he is one of them...

...Destroyed a whole world!

Kevin was so busy letting the arguments wash over him that he almost didn't hear the moment when the first person stood up.

"I speak for the boy," a woman said, in a gentle tone. "I feel that although he has done great wrong, he only did it when controlled by the Hive. When free, he sought to help us. He warned us. He broke free, and we should not reward that with harm. We should take him in as we did his friend."

"I speak against," a man said. "Whatever else is true, he *was* one of the Hive. They slaughtered more than we could count without our AIs, and he helped them. Am I supposed to watch him walk around freely, when those we love cannot, because they are dead? Are we supposed to forgive the unforgivable now?"

"I speak for the Purest," an older man said. "They are part of a whole, and he has broken from that whole. He was twisted by who he was, but he is not that creature anymore. If he has had the courage to break free from them, we should celebrate that, not denounce it."

"No one breaks free," another of the Ilari snapped, and the anger there was palpable. "It's obvious that this is some kind of trick. They tried to trick us before. They broke through our shields. They murdered our people. They destroyed our *world*. This thing was a part of that, they both were! We should destroy it before it harms us further."

Kevin could hear the emotion coming through there, completely different from the way the Hive had been. They would have made decisions purely rationally, while this… this felt more *real* somehow.

"Do you wish to speak for yourselves?" General s'Lara said, looking over to him and Ro.

Kevin knew that he ought to, but he wasn't sure what to say. The guilt he felt still seemed as though it flowed over everything, burying any words. He knew he had to try, but the truth was that he didn't *want* to try right then.

"I don't want to speak for myself," he said, shaking his head. "I don't deserve it, and the truth… I'm dying anyway. It doesn't matter what you do to me, so long as the others are safe." It almost came as a shock to hear himself saying it, but it was the truth. It was more important that Ro and Chloe were safe than that he was. "I helped to destroy a world. I don't deserve… I don't deserve anything, but Ro broke free from the Hive. That should count for something."

Ro shook his head. "I am… I am scared, I admit that, but I will not run from what I have done. I have committed horror upon horror. I have done evil things. Once I was Purest, but now, I am not even that. I am impure. It is Kevin you should save. We made him one of us against his will. He had no choice."

"There is always a choice!" the man who had spoken against Ro called out from somewhere in the back of the room.

Kevin didn't know what to say to that. It seemed that Chloe did, though, because she shouted above the rest of it, looking straight at the man who had spoken.

"You think Kevin *chose* to be taken over by aliens?" she demanded, in a tone that would have been enough to make most people take a step back. "You think he was in control? They made him say yes to hurting me in all kinds of ways, and even so, I don't blame him, because it *wasn't* him. It was him without any emotions, without any compassion. And if you don't have compassion, you're no better than the Hive!"

She took a moment to look around at the aliens, and for a moment Kevin thought she might be done, but then she kept going, jabbing her finger at the people around them.

"You're all standing there making decisions about us, but you haven't even *tried* to understand us. Kevin… he's been across our country trying to save our world. He's gone into space because he was trying to stop the Hive. They only took him because he was trying to stop them. As for Ro, he's fought back against everything he has ever known. He's a sign that the control of the Hive *can* be broken, and you want to… what, kill him? You'll have to kill me if you want to do that!"

She stood there glaring at them, and General s'Lara held up a hand for silence.

"I will not speak on this," she said. "My own thoughts are too conflicted. Logic demands one thing, emotion another. Yet I would ask, are we beings of pure logic? Are we like them? I don't know. It is time for us to divide."

She bowed her head, and above them, Kevin saw dancing lights buzz around as AIs talked and debated, presumably balancing the feelings of the Ilari with the needs of logic. To Kevin, they looked like swarms of angry bees moving around, shifting and splitting, then recombining in different combinations as the debate between them went on.

From down where he stood, Kevin couldn't begin to work out exactly which way the debate was going. He could catch snippets of it if he tried, but there were so many different fragments that even he couldn't begin to work out which way it was going.

Finally, something seemed to be happening. Kevin had the sense of the AIs shifting, moving into stacks, forming into groups as they made their decisions. Two blocks, one red and one blue, appeared on the surface around the edge of the room. The groups seemed close; so close that Kevin couldn't count them, and couldn't begin to guess which one was larger. He could see some AIs still buzzing around, reviewing the facts or discussing them with those they were connected with. Slowly, though, the count settled, and the groups stabilized.

Even then, Kevin couldn't guess at what the outcome was.

CHAPTER TWO

Kevin watched out of one of the ship's windows as space passed by in a blur, stretched and bent to let the ship pass through by the power of its shields. He, Ro, and Chloe sat together in a room that was open and airy and almost empty. To his surprise, General s'Lara was there too.

Kevin flashed back, recalling General s'Lara's hand on his shoulder, after the trial.

"We have made our decision. It seems... it seems that you will all be permitted to stay among us. You will be taken to our outpost world, and together, we will seek a way to stop the Hive. I just hope that we can find a way to do it."

Kevin could not believe how close they had come to death. He snapped out of it and looked around.

"Don't you need to… I don't know," he said, "be in charge of the ship?"

"As if my ship would let me tell it what to do," she said. "We work *with* our AIs. We do not enslave them. That is Hive thinking."

"Kevin and Ro aren't the Hive," Chloe said, hotly, maybe a little too hotly.

"I never said they were," General s'Lara said. She seemed to be watching Kevin and Ro carefully though.

Kevin thought he understood. "You're trying to learn more about the Hive, aren't you?"

The general hesitated, listening in that way that said she was in communication with her AI again.

"Yes," she admitted. "You and Purest… sorry, Ro here have been a part of it. You've had access to everything that it is. You can help us to understand it better. You might actually be able to help us beat them."

"I'm not sure they *can* be beaten," Ro said. "I'm sorry. I feel… hopeless."

"But you managed to break free," General s'Lara said.

"With Chloe's help," Ro replied.

Kevin nodded. Without Chloe, none of them would have been able to escape.

"I still want to know as much as you can tell us," the general said. "What is it like being a part of the Hive?"

Kevin wasn't sure that he had the words to explain it. Even so, he wanted to try. "It's like… there's this web of connections, and every one is a living thing. It's being a part of something bigger, and feeling that nothing matters but that whole."

"It's beautiful," Ro added. "But we have no way to feel that beauty. We feel nothing. No conscience, no happiness. The Hive is everything."

"Well, that means negotiating is out of the question," General s'Lara said. "Still, maybe there will be something. We'll be there soon."

"Where?" Kevin asked. He had no idea where they were heading; hadn't even considered that they had to be going *somewhere*.

She gestured, and one of the walls shifted, providing an image of a planet. It seemed small on the screen, but was a bright point of color in an otherwise black and white view of space. It was largely green, in a way that seemed strange compared to the blue of Earth.

"This is Xarath," the general said, by way of explanation. "Most of its water is underground, but the plant life comes up to the surface. We have a small base there. It was never intended to be a home for all of us, but we will have to make it one. I'm told that it is beautiful."

"How long until we reach it?" Kevin asked. He had no real sense of how fast the ship was moving. Was it as fast as the Hive ships? Faster?

"A few more minutes. We have been folding space to get closer for a while now, but most of the delay has been to try to lose the Hive forces tracking us. We will need to be some of the first onto the surface. Come with me, we should get to one of the landers."

For the second time, the general started to lead them through the inner workings of the ship. People turned to stare at them as they passed, and while some of them seemed to be waiting for orders from the general, others were definitely staring at Kevin, Chloe, and Ro. Not all of them seemed friendly.

"Looks like not everyone agrees with the trial," Chloe said. She sounded to Kevin as though she was ready to fight off anyone who looked at them for too long, or in the wrong way. He could see her altered hand clenching as if ready to punch someone.

"People get to disagree," General s'Lara said. "We are not the Hive, where everyone must obey. They can think what they like, but we have made a decision the fairest way we can, and I doubt anyone will act against it."

She didn't seem entirely certain to Kevin, but then, he thought, how could she? She was right. Unless they controlled every mind there like the Hive, there would be no perfect harmony. Kevin would rather have people giving him odd looks than have to live without his own thoughts, his own choices.

He and the others followed the general to a hangar where a number of smaller ships sat, looking like darts waiting to be spat out by the giant mouth of the ship. General s'Lara led the way to one that was partly blackened by fire.

"Here. My own craft. I'll show you the planet. Come on."

The inside of the ship was stranger than the outside. It looked as though it had been patched and rebuilt so many times that there was hardly anything of the original left.

"I worked on this one myself," General s'Lara said, and then did the glancing away thing again. "Yes, all right. *We* worked on it. Take a seat and we'll fly down."

There were chairs that looked more like armchairs than the kind of benches or flight seats that Kevin would have expected from a military craft. It seemed strange to have such comfort in a general's ship.

"What's it like being linked to an artificial intelligence?" he asked.

"It's like being two halves of a whole," the general replied. "They can provide more information, react faster, and work things out that I never could, but we provide the emotion and the intuition. It works."

Kevin tried to imagine it, and couldn't. The closest he could get was the connection to the Hive, and that had been nothing like the way General s'Lara described. It sounded more like a kind of perfect friendship, the way he'd had with Luna back on Earth, each of them filling in for the other's weaknesses, each of them looking out for the other without question.

He missed Luna so much right then that it hurt.

"Hold on," General s'Lara said, but in truth, the movement of the ship was perfectly smooth as it exited the larger vessel that held it, sliding down toward the surface.

As they descended toward the world below, Kevin could see the greenery ahead of them, so great that it seemed to encompass everything. For the first few seconds, it was just one giant wash of green, but then he started to make out different shades and textures within it. There were areas that appeared to be open grassland, and far more that seemed like nearly endless forests. There were patches of dark green similar to firs, and others that looked like tropical palms.

As they got still lower, Kevin started to get a sense of the scale of them. Many of the trees seemed to be normal sizes, but there were others that were as tall as cathedrals, and whose canopies spread out to cover huge swaths of land, so that the ground beneath seemed almost like an afterthought.

"It's a beautiful place," General s'Lara said. "So much lives here, but it was never intended to be a world for us. It is too wild, and too many of any species will upset its balance."

She took her ship down low, and Kevin could see buildings now, nestled amongst the trees, disguised so well that for a few seconds it was hard to pick them out from among the foliage. They hung like great fruit, or balanced in the branches, so beautifully constructed that they might have been a natural part of the forest.

"How many people do you have here?" Kevin asked.

"A few thousand. Not enough for a true civilization," the general replied. "Even with all the people we've brought with us… we're a shadow of what we were."

Vehicles shot between the trees, moving rapidly, high above the ground. More moved slowly at ground level, disguised by shifting fields of color that changed as they caught the light.

"Do you have weapons here?" Kevin asked. He had to hope that they would have something that might destroy the Hive.

"Some," General s'Lara said. "We like to be able to defend the places where we have bases, but the main defense we have is secrecy. This was always supposed to be a hidden place."

"But we're coming here now," Chloe pointed out.

"We're desperate," General s'Lara said. "We're out of people, out of places, out of everything except this. We'll hide here for as long as we can."

"And if the Hive finds us?" Kevin asked.

General s'Lara shook her head. "We lost them when we started to bend space. Even they can't track us at those speeds. Unless you know something we don't?"

There wasn't any note of suspicion there, but even so, Kevin felt as though he wasn't entirely trusted. He looked over at Ro, who shook his head.

"The Hive has stolen many technologies before, but they cannot track the Ilari. It was why they required you, to trace their signals. Without you…"

"Without me, they would never have been able to destroy the world they ran to," Kevin said.

General s'Lara shook her head. "There will be others who try to blame you for it, Kevin, but I do not. You were controlled, and we are safe now."

They flew forward, in amongst the trees, the ships finding their way between the trunks to land on great platforms that extruded from the side of the buildings amongst the trees. This close, Kevin could see that there was a whole city there.

The ship touched down and they stepped out. Inside the landing craft, surrounded by walls, there hadn't been the sense of space there, but now, Kevin could see just how high up it all was. It was high enough that the air felt thin and made his head hurt, while he stumbled unsteadily. His brain felt bewildered by the sheer height.

"Come on," General s'Lara said. "I announced that we were coming as we approached, and people will want to meet you. They're excited by the prospect of people who could break free from the Hive, and they think that you, Kevin, are very special."

"Now I'm feeling left out," Chloe said, but she didn't sound as though she meant it that much.

Kevin put a hand on her shoulder. "I think you're special."

"You are," General s'Lara assured her. "If you will let our scientists study you all, we will potentially learn so much."

Chloe looked worried by that. "I've had enough of being studied for a lifetime."

"We won't force you," General s'Lara said, and there was something understanding about her tone then. "It's your choice. Now, come on. I'll show you the base."

Inside, it was every bit as impressive to Kevin as it was outside. The corridors had the same impossible scenes on them as had decorated the inside of the ships, each one turned into a canvas that it seemed the Ilari's AIs could manipulate, since Kevin saw one of the blue-skinned aliens manipulating the wall into a strange kind of abstract work as they passed. He turned to look at them, offering a kind of bow to the general.

"Oh, stop it, Cler, you know I'm the one who should bow to you," the general said.

They kept going, and the general started to explain the buildings they passed through as they went.

"In theory, people take whatever rooms they need for whatever they're trying to do, and reshape them to suit, but there tend to be common areas to it all," she said. "There are living spaces on either side here, in pods branching off the main corridor. These spaces seem empty. You can have those."

Was it really as casual as that? They needed a room so they got one? She led the way into a big open living space with couches and beds set out around it. The whole place was empty and still, but didn't seem sterile in the way that Kevin knew from the Institute, and it lacked the precise opulence of the Hive's golden towers. It was comfortable instead, and felt as though it could easily be someone's home.

"So we just wander in and take a room?" he asked, leaning against a couch as a brief wave of exhaustion hit him.

"How else would you do it?" the general asked, sounding genuinely puzzled that there might be another way to do things. She gestured to an open slot on a wall. "This is where we get food. It will be a little slower for you since you don't have AIs, but you can still ask for what you want. Here, let me."

She paused for a moment in front of it, and a tray of food just… appeared. Steaming strands of blue mixed with what looked like red berries sat there.

"My AI tells me that *laxatha* should be safe for you to eat, and it's one of my favorites," she said. "Here, try it."

She set it out in front of them and sat down beside them, in a way that seemed strange for a general to do. Chloe was the first to taste the dish, and the surprised delight on her face told its own story.

"This is… good isn't enough. It's amazing. You have to try it, Kevin."

Kevin took a tentative bite, and was surprised by just how good the mixture tasted. There was only one question on his mind, adding a slightly strange note to the meal while they ate.

"General s'Lara," he said, "why are you here serving us food?"

"Because you're our guests," the general said.

"And that's very kind, but you could have sent someone to do all of this. Don't you have meetings and things you need to be at?" Kevin had met at least some important people, and he couldn't imagine them doing this. "Why *you*?"

General s'Lara nodded. "I'll admit that there are plenty of talks I should be having, but my AI is having at least some of them with others. Besides, here with you may be one of the most important places I could be right now."

Kevin didn't get it for a moment, but then frowned slightly as he did. "Because of everything that we might know?"

"I won't lie to you," General s'Lara said. "I think that you three may hold the key to this. We've been able to beat individual members of the Hive, we can do it easily when the numbers are equal, but the numbers are never equal. They just keep coming, and worse, they just don't care. They throw creatures at us, and they don't care if they're killed or not. How do you fight something that doesn't worry if it is going to die?"

Kevin wasn't sure he had an answer to that. He'd used that against the Ilari when they'd been fighting. He'd thrown ships at them, seeing their desire to live as a weakness to be exploited.

"It's the Hive's greatest strength," Ro said.

"The fact that you know them, and you were able to break free, might let us understand how to actually beat them. We might actually be able to *win* this war."

"But we don't know anything," Kevin said.

"You might not know what you know," the general said. "For a start, what do you know about this ability of yours?"

Kevin shook his head. "I hardly know anything. I hear signals, and I can translate them. I see things that need translating, and my brain just does it."

"And it's killing him for it," Chloe put in, sounding somber. Just the words had Kevin feeling sad about the prospect of the ticking clock that had restarted in his body.

"What do you mean, killing you?" General s'Lara asked.

Kevin started to answer, standing up as he did so. The pain hit him almost immediately, and he realized that the things he'd been experiencing as they landed had been a lot more than just the background symptoms that had been plaguing him since he'd come out from the Hive again.

He'd gotten so used to ignoring it that he'd done it even when his body had been trying to warn him that something wasn't right. Now it seemed that everything hit him at once. Dizziness overwhelmed him, spinning Kevin half around, so that he dropped to the floor in stages, putting out a hand to catch himself even while it started to twitch in the beginnings of a fit that seemed to wrack every inch of him.

Pain came with it, bursting inside his head in a supernova of agony. It felt like something broke inside him then, and he would have screamed if his mouth had still been under his own control. He'd felt himself lose control of his body before when signals had ripped through him, but this was different. This didn't hold the promise of a message or an answer; the only promise it seemed to hold was the blackness that lay beyond it, threatening to rise up and overwhelm everything.

Kevin could see Chloe, Ro, and General s'Lara beside him, their lips moving as they talked. Chloe looked as though she was shouting something down to him, but he couldn't hear any of it. It felt as though it was on the other side of a curtain, and slipping further away by the second.

He was dying, and there was nothing he could do about it.

CHAPTER THREE

Luna woke, blinking in the light, and even that was a surprise. When she'd slept, she'd expected to slide down into darkness and not wake up, consumed completely by the alien nanobots that were slowly taking over her body. Instead, she could still remember who she was, and where she was, and all the horrors that had struck the world.

It was only when her body stood without her thinking about it that she realized that something was wrong.

"No!" she screamed, but the scream just came out as a groan past lips that refused to move in response to her commands. They weren't hers anymore, not really. Someone else was pulling the strings that controlled her.

She looked around at the compound where they'd fought against so many of the transformed and the aliens, and Luna had the sense that it wasn't just her looking around in that moment. Other things were looking through her eyes, making decisions on her behalf, issuing commands without a thought for what it might do to her.

Luna fought against those commands as hard as she could, but it made no difference, just as it had made no difference the last time she had been one of the controlled. Instead, she stood like a prisoner in her own flesh while her body started to walk over to the others, held by walls made of her own muscles. She grabbed a long shard of metal that was as sharp as any machete or knife. If it cut into her hands, she didn't notice.

Luna didn't understand that. Before, the transformed had grabbed blindly at people and tried to convert them, stupid in the absence of direct control. This, though… this felt like someone was using her for something far more focused, something far more dangerous.

She stalked forward, and it was only as Luna did so that she realized exactly who she was heading toward. Ignatius, Cub, Barnaby, and Leon stood ahead—all the people the resistance to the invasion needed. The aliens were going to use her as a knife thrust at the heart of it all, aimed to kill the only people who truly knew how they might stop what the aliens had done. If the aliens could kill them, then who would truly know how the cure worked?

Luna tried to shout a warning, but it didn't do any good. No sound came out, and while the change in her eyes would be obvious by now to anyone who looked, no one was looking. They were all too busy trying to recover from the aftermath of the battle, patching wounds and trying to find enough food for people who hadn't felt thirst or hunger for days or weeks.

Then Bobby the sheepdog ran up, growled, and bit her.

Luna didn't feel it, because at this stage, she couldn't feel anything. She looked down at the dog, drawing back her leg ready to kick him, and Luna knew that she would, in spite of all the effort she put into holding herself back. Bobby danced back, snarling and growling, as surely as if she'd been a wolf troubling some ancient flock. Luna stepped toward him, lifting the long shard of metal now.

"Bobby, what are you doing?" Cub demanded, moving forward.

Luna turned toward him, slashing with the weapon that she held and managing to cut through the skin even as he danced back from the attack. She remembered this strength and this speed, but she'd never had the chance to use it to strike out at anyone before. She hadn't realized just how dangerous it made her.

"Luna, what's going on?" Cub demanded, dodging back from another blow. Luna saw him stare at her. "Oh no. *No!*"

Luna charged at him and the others with all the speed of her kind, breathing out vapor even though she knew it would do nothing to people already inoculated against the danger. A man got in her way and she cut him down with her shard of metal, shoving another man out of her path.

"She's transformed!" Cub yelled above the sudden chaos.

Then he did the unthinkable, and reached for a gun.

Luna was already lunging for him, shoving him back and knocking the gun from his hand so fast she could barely believe how quickly she was moving.

"Grab her!" Ignatius yelled above the chaos.

Luna struck out toward him, the need to obey the Hive besting any attempt to resist. Inside, she was screaming, but it only came out as a dull hiss. A dozen other people were on her in that moment. Luna shook one of them off, throwing him away with more force than she could have believed, and lashed out at another.

Even so, more people piled in, and for all her strength, all her ferocity, Luna found herself pinned between them. There were too many of them to fight. She breathed out vapor in what seemed like the futile hope that it would turn some of these creatures, these humans… and even as she thought it, Luna caught herself. She wasn't what the aliens wanted her to be. She wouldn't lose track of who she was.

"She's changed," Cub said, shaking his head. "She's gone. Luna's *gone*."

He still had the gun in his hand, and his hand seemed to be shaking now, as if he were wrestling with a decision. Luna could guess exactly what that decision was, and she hated it.

"Don't say that," Leon said. "She might still be in there."

Luna wanted to scream that she *was* still in there. She wanted Cub to see that she was still there, that… well, she didn't know what happened after that.

Instead, she saw Cub lift his gun.

"I know what it's like as one of those things. Even if Luna is in there, she won't be for long. It sucks away who you are."

"But she's there *now*," Leon said. "We can still save her. The blast—"

"The blast converted people all around it during the battle, but it didn't save Luna," Cub said. Luna could see tears in his eyes now. "She's gone, and now I have to do… I have to do the only thing that *can* be done."

Luna could guess what he was thinking: that this was the same as with his father, Bear; that there wasn't another choice; that he was sparing her from a fate worse than death. Even so, he was pointing a *gun* at her, and she hated it. How could he *do* that to her? How could he think, even for a moment, that it was the right thing to do?

"Wait!" Ignatius yelled, and he was the last person Luna would have expected to step between her and a gun. The chemist and former drug maker was nothing if not a coward.

"Get out of the way," Cub snapped back.

"We can still save her," Ignatius insisted.

"If she wasn't saved when the blast went out—"

"Because she was at its center. The eye of the storm!" Ignatius said. He didn't move aside. Luna hadn't expected him of all people to stand in the face of that kind of danger. "It doesn't mean that she can't be saved. We just need—"

"What? To recreate the blast?" Cub demanded, and Luna might have wanted to dry the tears in his eyes if not for the reason for them. "Recreate a random burst of alien energy tuned to just the right frequency when it hit the crystals? Do you think I wasn't paying attention to what you've been saying, Ignatius? If I thought there was a way…"

He pulled the trigger on his gun and Luna saw the dust at her feet kick up. Her controlled body didn't flinch, didn't even react.

"That was a warning, Ignatius," Cub said, and Luna could hear the certainty in his voice now. "*Move.*"

Luna tried to get her body to move so that Ignatius wouldn't be in the line of fire, but she was imprisoned both within her own flesh and by the hands of those who held her. They wanted this. They wanted to make sure that the most people were hurt.

"The blast let us overwhelm the nanites involved in the change for hundreds," Ignatius said, "but we can still come up with a cure for one person at a time. We just need to process it."

Luna saw Cub hesitate at that. It seemed to be the only thing that was enough to do it.

"You can *really* do it?" he asked.

"Not here," Ignatius admitted. "The damage from the battle is severe, but all I need is a lab with the right equipment, and a few specific pieces of machinery."

"And in the meantime, we all have to hold onto Luna to stop her killing us?" Cub asked.

"We can build something to contain her," Barnaby said. He already seemed to be working on it, holding up rough pieces of metal to the remains of a motorcycle trailer as if he could already see the way it fit together in his head.

"And she'll pull in all the aliens from a hundred miles around," Cub said.

Luna knew what he meant. The creatures controlling her would see everything through her eyes. They would know where to send more.

"We're going to do that all by ourselves," Ignatius said. "We owe her this, Cub, and I promise we can get her back."

Cub stood there, but Luna could tell that he'd made his mind up. Maybe she should have felt grateful that he wasn't going to kill her. Maybe she should have felt some pity for the tough decisions that he'd had to take already. Instead, all she could think of as he stood there was that he'd been going to kill her. He'd actually been going to *kill* her.

"All right," Cub said. He backed away. "All right."

Luna continued to snap and snarl, unable to help herself, while the people held her in place. She was everything that Cub feared she was, but she was more than that. She just didn't have any way to let people know. A little further over, Barnaby was working on the enclosure designed to hold her. It looked like a kind of cage, made out of parts scavenged from the wreckage of the battle.

It came together slowly, piece by carefully constructed piece. As quickly as it came together, Luna felt herself gradually falling apart. She could feel memories sliding away into the depths of her being in a way that felt all too familiar. She'd felt this before, the first time she had been transformed, fragments of herself lost whenever she looked away from them, impossible to grasp, impossible to hold onto, like darting fish slipping through her fingers.

The memories of her parents slid into a vague kind of knowledge, with Luna unable to recall a single moment with them, a single instant spent laughing at home or arguing about chores or even sitting down together to eat. Luna knew the facts of her life, but couldn't recall it. She couldn't truly remember what it had been like to be in school, or to sit and watch TV, or to be outside, or…

…Kevin's face came into her mind so sharply and perfectly that it might have been a photograph, and Luna clung to that image as tightly as she might have held onto a metal post in a hurricane. She wouldn't lose Kevin, wouldn't lose a single fragment of him. She wouldn't lose the moments that she'd spent with him. Those moments seemed etched into her, from being there with him at the NASA Institute, to fleeing to the bunker and hiding from the flow of the vapor, to trying to bring down the aliens together.

There was something brighter about those moments than the rest of it, somehow. They stood out in Luna's mind indelibly, and she managed to cling to them, holding onto thoughts of Kevin, and to all the things that she felt for him. That need, that love, seemed like a beacon in the dark that threatened to engulf her,

"Bring her this way," Barnaby called out, and Luna looked up to see that he had completed his holding cell, so quickly that it stood as a reminder of just how talented he was when it came to building things. It looked roughly made, but the metal was thick, and the gaps between the bars were small enough that even Luna wouldn't be able to slip out.

They carried her toward it, and her body fought even if Luna's mind hoped that the cage would be strong enough to hold her. She felt her foot connect with a man's jaw, her elbow slam into someone's stomach. She felt blows connect hard enough to bruise or break bones, and it didn't seem to make any difference. Most of the people carrying her now weren't members of the Survivors, or at least, Luna didn't think they were. Instead, they had the ragged look of the people who had previously been transformed. They seemed willing to help her even when the others were afraid.

They picked her up and flung her into the cage. Luna didn't feel the landing. Instead, she rose and stormed for the door, but even her unbridled speed wasn't enough to make it there before the metal slammed into place and the Survivors managed to lock it shut.

Luna threw herself against the bars, testing the strength of them. The pulsing instructions of the Hive told her to tear her way free and kill, to do as much damage as she could before they cut her down, but the metal didn't give way under her hands, even when she tore at the bars hard enough to make her fingers bleed. That should have hurt, but like everything else as one of those transformed, it seemed to pass in a dream, almost happening to someone else.

The only problem was that the someone else was her, and this would *really* hurt if Ignatius was right about being able to change her back.

"Where do we go to process what we found?" Leon asked Ignatius and Barnaby. "We just need a lab, right?"

Luna tried to look away. She didn't *think* the aliens were dragging knowledge of the Survivors from her, but she had no way of knowing. Cub was right about that much: she was a threat to the rest of them with every moment that she was able to see and hear. She could draw in hordes of the controlled as surely as a beacon.

"It can't just be any lab," Ignatius said. "We're going to need specific pieces of equipment. The university would have had them, but with the attack, I'm worried that they might be gone."

"Where then?" Leon asked.

Luna saw Ignatius shrug, and in that moment she knew that this was anything but certain. Ignatius had made the process of bringing her back seem so simple, but he obviously didn't actually know where to find what they were looking for. None of them did, and somehow, Luna suspected that she only had a limited amount of time before everything she was disappeared for good. Even now, she could feel the weight of the aliens' infection pressing down on her, crushing everything that she was. It felt as though there was a hand behind it, closing slowly on her and *making* that happen.

"There are spots that might have what we need," Barnaby said, pointing out over the city like a tour guide. "There are industrial buildings that way, and if we can find a chemical plant, it will have everything we need. Or we can go that way and look at more academic buildings. Or we can go deeper into the university and hope that something survived."

Leon thought for a moment or two. Luna knew what she would have chosen, wanting to get to the nearest option, even if it was the least likely. She wanted this done as quickly as possible, and not just because she didn't want to spend any more time than she had to as the thing she was. She knew that every moment she was like this was a threat to all of the others.

It seemed that Leon disagreed, though, because he pointed to the factory buildings.

"They're our best chance," he shouted to the Survivors around him. "Ignatius and Barnaby will tell you exactly what they're looking for. We need the right equipment to save Luna, and to save other transformed we find."

The group gathered around them. There were so many now; practically an army, although that would have implied that they all had some kind of discipline rather than just moving forward together because they wanted to. They marched forward in the direction of the waiting factories, going on foot now since the school bus wasn't going anywhere in the wake of the battle. They dragged Luna along on her trailer, its wheels squeaking with every turn, its frame bouncing with every jolt of uneven ground. She felt like an exhibit in a museum, or perhaps like a captive in some ancient war, put on display before her death.

I'm not going to die, she told herself, trying to get herself to believe it. She clung to the thought of seeing Kevin again, the only point of certainty while more and more of her started to slip away.

Their procession set off toward the factories, and Luna just had to hope that they would be in time, before she lost even the parts of herself that managed to cling onto thoughts of Kevin.

CHAPTER FOUR

Kevin was walking through places he knew, places he'd been. He was wandering around them in odd combinations that made no sense, drifting from one to another as smoothly as breathing. He was walking on the Hive world ship that he'd been to, and the streets shifted so that they became the streets of Mountain View, where he'd grown up. He walked through a door, and now he was in the Colombian rainforest, with military people all around him, ready to fight for the right to control the Hive's capsule.

Each step brought a different moment, shifting and changing so that it was hard to keep track of them all. He moved from moments in the signal chamber, deciphering the messages sent to the Earth, to the first instant when he'd seen people changing into monsters, knowing that they were too late to stop the invasion…

…to the instant when the doctor had told him he was dying.

Kevin became distantly aware of his body then, although it was so far away that he seemed to be floating above it. He could feel the pain in his head, so great that it felt as though it was exploding. The tremors in his body seemed to claim him so completely that it was impossible that he could be moving through any of these places.

He couldn't be, he knew. He was dreaming, he was remembering, and he was dying.

You shouldn't be told that you were dying when you were thirteen years old. He remembered thinking that, right back at the start of all this, in the office of the specialist. Now, nobody was telling him; he just knew it, as surely as he knew what a distant signal meant, or the sound of Luna's voice.

He could feel the progress of the disease within him. It had been halted for the brief period that he had been a part of the Hive, but it had been far too close to this moment when they had stopped it.

More moments slipped through his dreams: sailing along the coast with Chloe and Luna; being in the bunker, there together in one corner of the dormitory, for that one brief night when it had been safe. Kevin wasn't sure whether this was just a dream, or the thing he'd heard of where people's lives flashed before their eyes before they died, or something in between.

More pain flashed through him, this time seeming to clench around his heart and crush it, holding it still so Kevin couldn't feel it beat. It was the kind of pain he couldn't have believed existed; the kind of pain that seemed to encompass everything at once.

There were so many images in his dreams; so many things he'd done that he might never have had a chance to if the world had been a different place. If he hadn't had his power, would the Hive still have come? Would he have been all the places he had, seen all the things he had?

However much Kevin had done, it wasn't enough. He didn't want to die. He hadn't wanted to die at any point in this. It wasn't *fair*.

"Come on, you have to do something!"

The words seemed to come from a long way away, Chloe's voice drifting in through a thin gauze that was still far too thick to reach through.

"We are attempting to," a voice replied, and although Kevin didn't recognize the individual, he recognized the Ilari language. "If we'd had time to study what was happening with him…"

"There is no time," General s'Lara said. "Do what must be done."

"Wait," Kevin tried to say, but the words wouldn't come out. "What do you *mean*?"

Then pain hit him, and if he'd thought he'd known what pain was before, this was a hundred times worse. It seemed to run through every cell of him at once, burning and freezing, tearing at him and crushing. It was as though it was tearing him apart, atom by atom, and rebuilding them one after another. Each cell was subtly different, subtly changed, and now it felt like a cool wave running through him, transforming him as he went.

Blackness rose up for him again, but this didn't feel like the blackness of death. Instead, it felt soothing, and gentle, and pure. It wrapped around Kevin as surely as a blanket, and finally, he could feel his body again.

"You can open your eyes now, Kevin," General s'Lara said.

Kevin's eyes felt gluey and hard to open. He felt tired…

"Kevin," Chloe said, far less gently. "Wake *up*."

Kevin's eyes flashed open, and he saw the room around him, white walled and gentle seeming. There were blue-skinned aliens around him, in pristine uniforms that seemed familiar. It took him only another moment to realize that this was yet another hospital. He was spending far too much time in these places. General s'Lara was there, looking on with obvious concern. So was Ro, and it was even stranger seeing the expression on the face of an alien species that normally had no emotions.

Then there was Chloe. She stood over him, and Kevin could see that she had been crying, although now her tears seemed to be ones of joy rather than pain. She reached out for him.

"Kevin, I thought you were dead!" she said. "I thought…"

"*I* thought I was dead," Kevin said, trying to make a joke of it even though it was anything but that. He could still feel the pain that had been clamped around his heart, so crushing and dangerous and deadly. He'd truly thought that he was going to die. He'd thought about all the things he'd done, and all the things he was going to lose.

As Kevin looked over at Chloe, though, he felt a burst of shame, because it hadn't been *her* he'd thought of in that moment when he'd been so certain that he was about to lose everything—it had been Luna. It had been times with Luna that had come into his mind when he'd been thinking about moments from the past that mattered. It had been Luna's memory he'd grasped hold of and kept close to him in the moments when he was dying. It had been Luna, not Chloe, whom he'd been so afraid of losing. Just looking at Chloe now felt like a betrayal, even though it was something that he couldn't help.

"Kevin, what is it?" Chloe asked. Of course she'd seen it.

"It's nothing," Kevin said, dismissing the thought. Instead, he stood up and walked around the room, trying to assess how he felt, ready for his body to be weak and ready to collapse from the effort involved even in trying to move. He was actually a little surprised that the medical staff there let him, but maybe they wanted to test how he was too.

Instead of collapsing he felt… healthy. Kevin wasn't sure he'd ever felt that healthy, at any point in his life. He could breathe easily, and there was no pain in his head, no tightness in his chest. It was only because all the things that had been wrong with him were gone that he was able to realize just how bad the sickness had been.

It felt as though there had never been a day of his life before this when he had been truly well, because this wellness felt almost alien compared to everything that had gone before.

"Are you sure you're all right?" Chloe asked him, and Kevin nodded. He wasn't sure how he could describe it.

"I don't think I've ever felt this good," he said. He looked around at General s'Lara and the medical staff, who all seemed to be looking over at him as if trying to check that things were working as they should. "What did you do?"

"We cured you," the general replied. "We scanned your body, searching for defective patterns, and then used our healing technology to overwrite those patterns with something new. Your brain has been stabilized, so that your illness cannot progress."

"And my ability to translate signals?" Kevin asked, and then realized the answer to that question before any of the others could say anything. The Ilari weren't speaking his language, but their own. He could still understand them, could still sense the signals of the AIs communicating with one another, and could still translate them when they got too loud.

...appears to be fully recovered...

...may be necessary...

"The procedure should have affected nothing but your illness," General s'Lara said, with a glance across to one of the medical staff, who nodded. Kevin could see her relief at that confirmation.

Kevin should have felt joy at that. He *did* feel joy, but there was more to it than that. He felt as though this should have been harder somehow. After all the work that scientists had done on Earth trying to stabilize and heal him, it felt impossible that these aliens could just make him well with so little effort.

"You... healed me," he said. "*Why*? Why did you heal me? You know what I did. You know I'm responsible for the destruction of the world you hid on."

"And we tried you for that," General s'Lara said. "We agreed to let you stay. Do you think we would hold back our healing from you when we had the ability to help you? That is not who we are. It is not *right*."

The sheer goodness and benevolence of that overwhelmed Kevin in that moment. How could these aliens be so benevolent? It seemed impossible that anyone could be so generous to someone who had done so much to hurt them. After all that he'd done...

"It wasn't your fault, Kevin," Chloe said.

Kevin wished he could believe that. All he could do was feel amazing levels of gratitude that the others felt that way.

"Thank you," he said to the general. "I... I don't know what to say."

They'd given him back his life. They'd healed him, when no one else could do it, and they'd done it when he was sure they had every reason not to do it.

"You don't need to say anything," General s'Lara said. "We help those who truly need it. We seek peace where it can be found. We *forgive*."

That seemed impossible to believe. Kevin wasn't sure he would be able to manage to forgive the Hive. If he had a chance to destroy it, then he would. And yet... he looked across to Ro. Kevin didn't hate him. He even trusted him, and yet the former Purest had been one of those trying to destroy his planet.

"I have so much to learn," Kevin said.

He looked across to Chloe, and again, he had the feeling of guilt that he'd been thinking of Luna and not her when he'd been dying. Chloe had been the one who had been there with him on the Hive's world ship. She'd helped him to escape. He knew what she felt about him, and he even felt some of it too… but it was Luna whose face was there when he shut his eyes, Luna he thought about in every spare moment, even though there was every chance that she was lost in the mass of the transformed.

"You've been given a fresh start, Kevin," General s'Lara said, gently, as if she understood the sheer enormity of everything that was happening for Kevin. "The question is what you choose to do with it."

Kevin couldn't stand there in the room right then. It was too much. It wasn't just that he didn't know what to say, or what to think. He wanted to breathe the open air in that moment. He wanted to remind himself that he was actually *alive*. That he could actually potentially have a future.

There were doors from the medical bay leading out onto a kind of balcony that appeared to have been grown from the tree itself. It curved around like some great fungus growing out of the trunk, more than big enough to hold him and a dozen others. Kevin stepped out onto it, the trees surrounding him, the beauty of the world spread out below. Here and there, small ships darted between the trees as agilely as birds, or up to the larger vessels in orbit. Birds bigger than Kevin nested in some of the branches, singing songs that filled the space with music, while creepers hung down almost to the ground, and furred creatures half Kevin's size clambered up and down them.

The air was sweet out there, and it wasn't just the musk of forest flowers and the leafy canopy, although that helped. It was the fact that he could take a full breath without pain, and stand there without the dizziness that came from his leukodystrophy threatening to overwhelm him. It was so strange standing there like that, and the longer Kevin did it, the more certain he was that his whole life had been affected by this disease. He'd *thought* that it had only come into his life in the last few months, but one breath of the air here told him that it had always been a part of him, lurking and waiting, only seeming to come to life at the point where it got too bad to deal with.

He stood there looking out at the enormity and the beauty of the world around him, and the sheer emotion of it all felt simply overwhelming. So much had happened to him, and now, he felt healthier than he had ever felt. Even so, he felt tiny against the scale of it all. He felt as though there were too many things that he didn't know; too many things that he still needed to learn and understand. He had all of this new life to spend, and there was so much to learn and do in it that even now, he didn't know if it would be enough.

"Kevin, are you all right?" Chloe asked, coming out after him.

For a moment or two, Kevin wanted to hide behind the strangeness of everything that he had experienced. He wanted to tell her that it was just about the shock of what had happened, or about the sudden healing. He wanted to pretend that everything was all right. He wanted to lie, even though Chloe was the one person who deserved so much better than lies.

He knew he couldn't, though.

"I… Chloe, there's something that I have to tell you."

"You love Luna," Chloe said. She stood there, still as a statue, not saying anything, obviously leaving it until Kevin was willing to say something. It took him a moment, simply because of the shock of Chloe beating him to it.

He nodded. "I… she's been my friend forever. I think about her all the time. I wish… I *wish* I could feel that way about you, but I don't."

Chloe stood there for what seemed like forever, and Kevin found himself wishing that he hadn't inflicted this kind of pain on her, even as he knew there hadn't been any other choice. He didn't want to hurt her, but he didn't want to lie to her either. Kevin waited for her to explode at him, shout at him, react with all the emotion that he knew filled her to the brim. Instead, she just stood there, as still as a statue.

"Yes," she said at last. "I know."

"You know," Kevin said. "That's it?"

"What do you want me to say?" Chloe shot back, and Kevin could hear the pain there now. "It hurts, of course it hurts, but I saw in the Hive how much worse things could be. I saw how evil it is to try to force what I feel onto people. I…"

Kevin could see the tears building in her eyes, and he put his arms around her automatically, holding her close to comfort her. He was pretty sure that the person who had just told you they didn't love you shouldn't be the one to comfort you for it, but he did it anyway.

"I'm sorry," he said. "I wish—"

"What do you wish, Kevin?" Chloe asked. "That none of this had happened? Don't wish that. I don't."

A part of Kevin did wish it, in spite of that. He wished that the alien invasion had never happened. He wished that he hadn't opened the capsule they'd sent, or that he'd been able to do something to stop the damage that had been done. He couldn't count the number of people who had been hurt, or worse, because of the things that he had done. If he could take those things back, he would, simply because Kevin hated the pain that was in the universe because of him. Yet, if that hadn't happened, he would never have met Chloe. He would never have done half of the amazing things that he had done.

Kevin knew then that Chloe was right: he shouldn't wish that things were different. Even so, he was still contemplating how to answer that when he saw the skies starting to darken, an all too familiar shape moving into place above the world.

"No," he whispered. "No…"

The Hive world ship moved into place like some kind of trick of the eye, one moment not there, the next there. It hung above the Ilari world, dominating the skyline, ships already starting to pour down from it, making it look as if it were easy to move something so huge and terrifying.

Kevin saw General s'Lara rush out onto the balcony with the same horror that he felt in that moment. They'd thought that they were safe. They'd thought that they had time, at least.

"How?" she asked. "How did they find us when we lost them?"

She looked from Kevin to Chloe, and back toward where Ro stood within the medical bay. Her suspicions were obvious to Kevin, and it was hard not to share them. Not that he thought for a moment that Ro would have done anything deliberately, but what if there was some residual connection to the Hive? What if they were tracking Kevin, and not Ro?

He was still thinking that when Chloe moved forward, holding up her arm.

"It… it's pulsing. I think… I think they're tracing it. Get it off me. Get it *off*!"

Kevin didn't want to know what to say then. Above them, the world ship held its place, raining down smaller ships with the promise of death. Kevin looked up at them, feeling the sheer unfairness of it all. The Ilari had just saved him, had just given him the chance to live out the rest of his life.

Now the Hive was here, and Kevin couldn't see any way that they weren't all going to die.

CHAPTER FIVE

Luna was… Luna *was*. She had to try to remember that. She had to remember that she existed, and was real, and was not just… just… no, the memory and the words were slipping away even as she and the rest of the… the *Survivors*, that was it, made their way toward the factories that they'd picked out as the likeliest spot to have the things they needed.

Luna raged against the inside of her cage, tearing at the steel as if her hands might be able to rip through it. She could see the blood on the bars now, and she couldn't even remember where it had come from. Was it her attacking the metal, or was it something else? She tried to stop herself, but she had no control over her body. The aliens who had control of her wanted her to find a way out of there, to find a way to kill, no matter how much it damaged her in the process.

"Hold on, Luna," Ignatius said. Even he sounded worried now. "We're going to find a way to process the cure. We're going to bring you back to yourself."

It wasn't herself that Luna was thinking of in that moment, though. She was thinking of Kevin instead. Kevin was the one whose memory she held onto the way a climber held onto rocks for fear of falling. She clung to his image, but now even memories of him were starting to fade, as ragged around the edges as a… as a… she couldn't remember what. She *could* remember traveling across the country with him. She could remember the fun times before all of this had started, when they had still just been friends, but so much of what had come in between had started to slip away. Even so, she clung to Kevin as tightly as she could, and by doing that, she seemed to cling to some of the rest of it. She recognized Bobby the dog running amid all of it, staying as close as he could to her. He wasn't growling now, but maybe that was because he recognized that she couldn't hurt anyone.

They were approaching the factories now, and Luna could see the others looking around with the kind of obvious caution that came from too many bad experiences. There were so many of them now; practically an army, and a part of Luna said to her that she should be trying to make them into things like her. She breathed out gas at them even now, though it had no effect, thanks to the cure.

Some of them looked at her with fear as they walked, as though expecting her to hurt them at any moment. Some fingered weapons, as if unsure whether to use them. She recognized one of the ones doing it as being named Cub, but she couldn't remember anything else about him then, or why it hurt so much that he was one of the ones closing his hand around the butt of a gun.

"Looks as though this place has been the site of a few battles," Ignatius said, turning to Leon. "Are you sure they'll have what we need to process ore?"

Leon shrugged in response, and that was a long way from comforting to Luna. "I'm not sure of anything. There have been sounds of fighting around the factories, and the transformed might have scavenged. We don't know what's here."

Luna didn't know what to think about that. In truth, she could barely think at all by that point. In spite of Leon's reservations, the group pressed forward cautiously among the remains of the factory buildings, looking around them as they went as if searching the shadows for enemies. The whole place looked as skeletal now as the carcass of some great creature made of steel, portions of walls damaged or even collapsed in whatever fighting there had been around there.

They took her on her juddering cart through into a space where the sign for a chemical company hung at an angle, looking as though it might fall at any moment. Vats and canisters stood wherever Luna looked, some large enough to be crossed by walkways of perforated metal. A few of the vats looked empty now, looted or leaking or just evaporated, but several rippled with chemicals, bubbling here and there in ways that promised death for anyone unlucky enough to fall in. Debris littered the floor so that it was hard to pick a way between it, from girders that looked as though they had fallen from the ceiling, to boxes scattered here and there that looked as though they had been searched for their contents.

The Survivors spread out around Luna, starting to search the factory, moving between the piles of debris and picking through what was left, presumably in the hope that one of them would contain something useful.

"What are we looking for?" one of them called over.

Barnaby answered that one. "We're going to need machinery for processing chemicals into a usable form. Not the vats. Look further back."

All Luna could do was wait and hope, and she hated the waiting. Part of her hated it because it meant that she couldn't kill any of the people around her, but Luna knew that part wasn't really her, just the part that was controlled. The bigger worry was that the more time passed, the harder it was to remember that. She couldn't wait, because there was no *time* to wait.

"Here!" Leon called, from behind a pile of junk. There was a noted of hope in his voice, but Luna didn't dare to share it right then. "Barnaby, Ignatius, come look at this."

Luna saw the two of them disappear behind the same pile. Seconds passed, then minutes.

"Bring Luna," Ignatius called out, and his hope felt somehow more solid, because he knew what it was they were looking for.

The figures around her wheeled her forward, across the roughness of the factory's floor. Through the bars of her cage, Luna saw machinery she didn't understand, but some of it seemed to be designed to grind, while parts of it scanned and parts of it liquefied. From the scuff marks on the floor, it seemed that Barnaby and Ignatius had dragged a couple of parts of it closer to one another in order to lash pieces of it together, while a couple of smaller pieces of equipment had been duct taped together to make a larger whole, albeit an unsteady one.

The two of them were working on the ore, and, from the way Luna threw herself at the bars even harder then, she guessed that they were achieving something. She kept going until—

"Stop!" a voice ordered, and it sounded like a voice used to giving orders and having them obeyed. "Stop, right now!"

Men and women came out of hiding places around the factory. All of them held guns that looked far more sophisticated than anything the Survivors had. Most of the people there looked as though they knew how to use them too, moving smoothly, aiming accurately, and not betraying a hint of concern as they surrounded Luna and the others.

"What are you doing here?" the man in the lead demanded. He had a pistol leveled at Luna. "Why have you brought one of those *creatures* here?"

"Luna isn't a creature," Leon said, obviously deciding to take charge. "She's our friend, and she saved all of us. We just need—"

"You just need to *leave*," the man said, "and you need to do it at once. I am Captain Harris of the Seventy-fifth. I have kept my people alive through discipline, and by making the choices that have to be made. I will not allow looters in our area, and I will kill the alien scum on sight!"

There was a crack as he fired, and Luna heard the ping as the bullet ricocheted off the metal of her cage, close enough that she was sure she could feel it passing close to her. Weirdly, she didn't flinch or feel afraid, although perhaps that was because the progress of the alien vapor within her.

Around Luna, the guns of the Survivors came up, along with all the weapons held by the rest of the people they'd saved. The figures above had the more advanced weapons, but there were far more of those below, and plenty of them looked ready to fight and die if they had to.

They're ready to fight to defend me, Luna thought, a little shocked by it. She hadn't thought that so many people would ever do something like that for her. She hadn't thought that—

"I've got it!" Ignatius yelled, running forward, and even Luna knew that running forward was a mistake in an instant like that.

In that moment, another shot rang out, and Ignatius stumbled, clutching at his leg. Luna could see the blood, and if she'd had any kind of emotions, maybe she would have been worried by that. Around Luna, more shots sounded, and people screamed, while more ran to try to get into cover. If she'd had any control of her body right then, Luna might have pulled back toward the far side of the cage, but she couldn't, and she stood there as still as a statue. The fighting sounded around her regardless.

She saw Ignatius crawling across the floor toward her, despite all of it. He crawled with a look of determination that seemed completely out of place on his features. Ignatius didn't do that kind of thing. He turned and he ran, but here he was, crawling to her in spite of the pain of a bullet wound. Luna's hands reached out toward him, but not trying to help. She felt herself reaching for him, trying to hurt, trying to kill.

He got close to her and she tried to swipe at him, only for him to jab her with something that he held. Luna couldn't feel the needle going into her flesh, but she could see it, and seeing it, she had a moment to feel hope before her fist smashed into Ignatius and sent him sprawling back.

This would work; it had to. Luna wanted to believe that she could feel whatever Ignatius had just done to her spreading through her body, fighting the alien control. She wanted to believe that…

The pain hit her, suddenly and completely, ripping through her, tearing at her. Luna screamed, and somehow the scream cut through the violence, bringing it to a halt simply because everyone there was too busy staring at her to do anything else. She wanted to look around at them, wanted to say something, but her throat still wouldn't open for her words, and her body still wouldn't do what she wanted.

Instead, she collapsed like a sheet dropped from waiting hands.

Luna saw Kevin. She saw him standing atop a world ship identical to the one that had hung above Earth, looking so dangerous and blank-eyed that he might as well have been one of the creatures himself. She saw golden towers and creatures there... saw the power building within it.

She saw the Earth torn apart by that power, layer by layer. Luna watched as energy poured into it, tearing off the atmosphere, ripping apart the plates that held the world together. She saw it explode, leaving nothing but rocks behind.

Luna saw Kevin again. This time, she found herself thinking of the times she'd spent with him on the road, and in the bunker, on the ship, and traveling by bike with him in the sidecar. She'd been clinging onto the image of his face as a way to hold onto the past, but now, all of the past with him was there for her to claim, laid out as if waiting for her to inspect it.

She saw every moment that she'd spent with Kevin set out in front of her, all of them at once, all visible as perfectly as if they'd been caught on camera. She could see the first moment they had met, and the look on his face in the first seconds when she'd been turned into something controlled by the aliens. She could see the first time he'd gone to her house, and all the many times that she'd been to see him, clambering over fences, slipping in without bothering with anything so boring as a path.

Luna knew that she was dreaming, but the dreaming wouldn't stop just because she knew about it. Not even when it turned darker. Luna saw moments then that had nothing to do with her memories. She saw walls of the controlled, marching in step, descending on an army of humanity. She saw people being torn apart, ripped limb from limb by the mindless hordes.

She saw worse things: monsters that had never been human; things with tentacles instead of feet, and bodies made of brittle plate. She saw a battle that made her want to scream in terror even though she refused to look away. She couldn't have even if she'd wanted to, though, because the dream wouldn't let her.

It made her watch while Kevin stood in a room, watching the deaths of worlds. She saw him as a part of the Hive, and then striding across the world. She saw death after death, in place after place. She saw him coming toward her, and because she was still controlled, she had no choice but to move toward him, standing there as he reached for her, ready to kiss her...

Luna gasped as she woke, lying on the floor of the cage with her heart hammering in her chest as if it might tear through it and burst into the room beyond. She hurt. She hurt more than she had ever thought that she could hurt. It was so much that a part of her wanted to curl up into a ball and just go back to sleep. The nightmares would be waiting for her again, though, if she did that, and Luna couldn't bear the thought of that last one, where Kevin had been looking at her with such dead, expressionless eyes. That had been almost worse than seeing the world destroyed.

Almost.

Instead of lying there, Luna balled up that horror and that need to escape from the dreams, using it to force herself up to a sitting position, ignoring the way her body hurt. Her hands hurt. Her ribs hurt. Everything hurt, and Luna groaned with it. From sitting, she made it to her hands and knees, and from there, she pushed her way back to her feet.

Around her, Luna saw people staring at her, from both her side and the people who had been firing down at them. It took her a second or two to remember who they all were, because it seemed as though they were all from some other, earlier life. They stared at her in silence, as if waiting for something, wondering something. Even Ignatius did, sitting up with his back to one of the chemical tanks.

It took Luna a moment to realize what it was they were waiting for.

"I'm not controlled," she said, her voice feeling hoarse after everything that had happened to her. Just speaking seemed to scratch at her throat, but she forced herself to raise her voice anyway. "I'm not controlled! I'm human, and the cure works!"

"How do we know that this isn't some trick?" Captain Harris demanded from above.

"You know it because most of the people here were once controlled too!" Luna shouted, trying to hold back her anger at this man who had dared to fire down at them. She knew he'd just been trying to protect his people, and that bought him at least a little leeway. "We have found a cure, and the cure is our greatest weapon against the aliens."

She looked around again, seeing the men and women who were injured or dead around her. She wasn't sure how many of each there were, only that every one who had died was one too many. Above her, she could see the people who had attacked them still standing ready, as if they expected the fight to resume at any moment.

"Get me out of this cage," she called over to Barnaby, who she was glad to see was still safe nearby. Better yet, Bobby stood next to him, the dog apparently just as unharmed. Luna had been afraid for both of them, and for everyone else.

Barnaby started over toward her, and Luna saw Captain Harris raise his weapon above her.

"If you let the girl out, I'll shoot you both," he called down.

"And give the aliens just what they want," Luna called back, annoyed now. She'd let him get away with everything he'd done so far, but this was too much. She gestured to Barnaby, who kept coming, unlocking the cage so that Luna could step out. The others around her stepped back, and Luna couldn't quite tell if it was just awe at what had happened, or some residue of fear that she might still be a monster, there to try to kill them.

Bobby, at least, seemed happy about who she was. He ran over to her, nuzzling up against her until Luna ran a hand through his fur. She stood there, reveling in the softness of it, and in the fact that she could *feel* it. She took the moment to look back up at Captain Harris.

"Well?" she demanded, trying to sound brave after everything that had happened, trying to sound *certain*. "Aren't you going to shoot me?"

She could see the hesitation in the soldier's face, and she pressed on, wanting to take advantage of it before he could make up his mind another way.

"We need to stop this," Luna said. "We need to stop fighting each other. Our world has been taken, but instead of fighting back, we have spent our time fighting over the scraps. That has to stop today! We have to work *together*."

She wasn't done. Luna could have pulled back, but instead, she walked forward, toward the soldier, her hands outstretched. She tried to ignore the faint trickle of blood where she'd obviously gripped her piece of metal too hard, or tried too violently to get through the bars. Instead, she just kept walking. They could have shot her in that moment, could have killed her easily, but somehow, Luna knew that they wouldn't.

"We have a cure that works," she said, wanting them to hear it as many times as possible. "I have seen what the material we found can do. With the right energy, it can send out waves that cure people, and even take the aliens' creatures from their control."

She paused, hoping that she'd judged this right.

"We can win this, but we need your help. Something worse is coming. Worse than the controlled; worse than the vapor and the gangs and the rest. If we don't act, and act now, the world could be destroyed!"

CHAPTER SIX

Kevin saw the swarm of alien ships descending from the sky and looked over at Chloe, not knowing what to say. She still looked horrified, scrabbling at the living augmentation fused with her left arm, trying to tear it away. Kevin put his arms around her.

"Chloe, this isn't your fault," he said. "This isn't because of you."

"If not me, then who?" Chloe demanded, pulling back from him. She gestured with her altered arm. "I'm the one they can track. I should… I don't know, just get in a ship and fly away from all of you."

"Don't you dare," Kevin said. "They did this *to* you, Chloe. You didn't choose it."

"Not choosing things makes it worse, not better," Chloe said, and Kevin should have guessed that she might say that. She shook her head, looking as though she might cry.

General s'Lara was there then, looking up at the sky beside them. "They're here. I thought that we would have more time. I *hoped* that they wouldn't find us."

"It was me," Chloe said, holding out her arm. "I don't want you thinking that Ro did this or anything, because they tracked *me*."

"It isn't your fault," the general said. "We scanned your arm and found no danger in it. We should have considered that there might be something we couldn't see before we got anywhere near to the planet, and found a way to block it." She shook her head. "But that's done now. We have to focus on what's happening, not on what might have been. Can the three of you fight?"

Kevin didn't know if he had a good answer to that. He wasn't sure that there was one, when no one he knew of had managed to defeat the Hive. "We've… survived the aliens before, I guess."

"And you?" she asked, looking across to Ro, then up to where the sky was filling with smaller ships, some firing down at the ground, some looking as though they were trying to get close enough to land. "Can you fight against your own people?"

"I am impure now, not Purest," Ro said. "They are no longer my people. I am a horror to them, and they to me. I will fight if it means defending people from the horrors my people inflict."

"Good," General s'Lara said. "Because my guess is that soon, we will need every person on this planet to do their part. Come with me."

She turned and led the way from the balcony, out through the room, and into the corridor. The sense of peace and harmony that Kevin had experienced there before had gone now. The shifting walls all flashed with alarm colors, and arrows telling groups of people where to go, the artwork there long gone in the face of the emergency. General s'Lara led the way to a strong-looking door, flanked by turrets that seemed to have popped up from the floor. Kevin saw the flicker of one AI talking to others, and then the doors slid open to admit them.

Within stood an armory, stocked with more weapons than Kevin could have believed the Ilari might have had. There were long, rifle-like weapons, and shorter pistols, things that fit over hands like gloves, and what appeared to be jumpsuits just a little heavier than the silvery ones the aliens had put him, Chloe, and Ro into.

"Find a suit that fits you," General s'Lara said. "There should be enough different ones to find suits for all of you."

"What are these?" Kevin asked. "Flight suits? Are we going to be flying ships?"

General s'Lara shook her head. "Among the trees, only those with an AI running things would be able to plot out a course, and that's where we plan to fight them, rather than up in open space where they have the advantage. These are armor suits."

They didn't look like armor to Kevin, and he could see Chloe looking confused too.

"They have built-in fields and absorption skins that should stop most things," General s'Lara promised. "They will limit damage from the Hive's attacks, but remember that the shields are not infinitely strong. There's no time to waste, though; get ready. Already, some of them are starting to land on some of the outer platforms."

Kevin grabbed one of the suits and dragged it on. It seemed to shrink in toward him, holding tight to him. There was a hood to pull up over his head, so he did so.

"The suit will defend against falling as well," the general said, "and will provide communications connections to the rest of us."

Kevin could hear that now, in the form of hundreds of different voices, and streams of chatter that could only be from the AIs. He understood all of it, all at once. He could hear General s'Lara giving orders and reviewing events even as she stood there in front of them. The others didn't seem to be hearing as much, and Kevin guessed that only his talent was letting him do this. He could see the battle through the constant streams of information, and he had to concentrate to filter it out.

"Here," General s'Lara said. "You'll need weapons."

She passed a long rifle to Ro, then handed Kevin a shorter, stockier gun. To Chloe, she handed a fat pistol, along with a long stick that crackled with energy.

"All of these are beam weapons," she said. "Point them and fire. Kevin, yours will fire rapidly if needed. Chloe, your pistol has more of a kick to it than it might seem. Remember that each weapon will need to recharge after too many shots. Watch the power bar on the side."

She grabbed a weapon for herself, looking worried as she checked that the energy rifle was functioning.

"There's a group coming this way," she said. "We will need to deal with them."

"What I don't get is why they don't just stand off and attack from orbit," Chloe said. "I mean, we've all seen what that world ship can do."

Kevin had seen it, far too close. He'd seen the whole process of it, but he'd also been a member of the Hive just long enough to understand why they didn't just destroy this world.

"The weapon will take time to recharge its power," he said. "And they don't care enough about their troops to worry about how many they lose trying to do things this way. Besides, it gives them another world to strip for resources once they've killed or converted everyone."

"Speaking of time," General s'Lara said, "we have to hurry. Go in the spots I point you to."

She picked out spots in the corridor's doorways, and Kevin could hear her AI going through options with her, showing her the likely consequences of each one. He could see her trying to find an option that would minimize the danger to the three of them, and Kevin could see only one problem with that: it left the general far too exposed.

Kevin knew that he couldn't let the Ilari general risk herself like that, and not just because she was far too important to the battle. After everything he had done, he hated the thought of anyone else dying for him.

Without asking, Kevin picked one of the options that left the general a little safer and moved to that spot.

"What are you—" General s'Lara demanded, but then looked to a turn in the corridor and raised her weapon, ready to fire.

Creatures came around the corner, almost too fast to follow. Kevin had seen some of them before, but the sheer mass of teeth and claws, spikes and fangs made him shudder.

The others were already firing. General s'Lara shot in bursts, bringing down one creature after another, while Ro fired from close to the back, picking off what seemed like the most dangerous of the beasts. Chloe shot with her pistol, and then, as one of them got close, stepped in and struck at it with her energy baton.

Kevin fired now too, feeling the kick of the weapon against him as it released burst after burst of energy. He half expected it to knock him over, but he felt stronger now than he ever had, and he held the weapon steady. He tried to pick his shots, but there was only so much he could do, when this was the first time that he had ever fired something like this. Maybe that was the reason General s'Lara had given him something that fired in bursts—so that he could actually hit something. He did. Creatures fell in front of him, and yet more came. Some of them had energy weapons of their own now, or weapons that used gravity technology to fire darts and balls at impossible speeds.

Kevin ducked back, but even so, he saw a flare of light as something glanced off his suit's shield. For a moment, he wondered if he'd made the right decision, putting himself in danger to make sure the general wasn't at risk, but then he threw himself back into the fight, firing again and seeing more of the alien creatures fall.

Then the turrets opened up, cutting down the rest of the foes in the corridor, scything them out of the way in a wash of energy. They were precise about it too, shooting between him and the others in a way that suggested that they were controlled by some kind of intelligence.

"We need to get moving," General s'Lara said. "It won't be long before more of them come, and we need to get to the space we have designated as the control center."

She ran along the corridor. Kevin nodded over at Chloe.

"Are you all right?"

"I'm fine," Chloe said. She clutched her energy stick tighter. "The more of them I get to bring down, the better."

Together, they and Ro ran after the general, and again, it was kind of a surprise to Kevin that he could keep up. He wasn't used to feeling this okay; more than okay. Even as a little kid, it now felt as though his body had been holding him back. When the Ilari had cured him, they'd given him this feeling, and far more. Of course, if he found himself killed in the middle of a battle, that wouldn't count for much.

Briefly, Kevin glanced out of one of the windows to track the progress of the battle beyond. Ships darted through the sky, weaving in and out of the trees, then turning loops in the air. As when he'd seen them fight before, it seemed that the Ilari ships had the advantage one on one, but the problem was always numbers. The Hive was happy to send more ships, lose more creatures, because nothing less than the Purest mattered to them.

"Quickly," the general called out. "We're almost there."

Ahead, Kevin could see a set of double doors, sealed shut against an encroaching horde of enemies. Some of them wore insectoid armor and carried guns, while one, at the center, shone in golden armor.

"One of the Pure has come into battle," Ro said. "They seek to advance themselves by showing their worth, or they want the pick of the spoils."

"Or they want us," Kevin guessed.

Ro nodded. "We would be a prize worth them coming to fight for. They rarely do so without the promise of such a thing."

"Well, it's time to remind them why not," General s'Lara said, detaching something from her belt and then throwing it in the direction of those clustered in front of the door. "Get down!"

Kevin threw himself flat, seeing Chloe and Ro do the same. He did it just in time. A wave of heat and energy washed out from where the general had thrown the grenade, leaving a cloud of smoke and the scent of burning in its wake.

Figures stepped from that smoke. Not many, but the ones in black armor and the single figure in gold were among them. They started firing, and Kevin had to roll out of the way as weapons fire hit the spot where he had been. He fired back and his weapon's energy slammed into the black armor of one of the creatures there, slowly punching a hole through it to whatever lay beneath before the creature collapsed.

Around Kevin, the others fired too, and they succeeded in bringing down foe after foe. One of the armored aliens ran forward, and Chloe leapt to meet it, her energy baton sparking as they exchanged blows. Kevin leapt in to join the fight…

…and found himself facing the golden-armored figure.

It held a kind of staff, from which energy flashed, flickering past Kevin as he dodged. The alien swung it at Kevin's head then, and he swayed back, kicking out at the creature and catching it in the abdomen. It fell away from him and he started to raise his gun, but it struck with the staff at full length, catching the end of Kevin's weapon and sending it spinning. The Purest leapt back into the fray, striking out at Kevin again and again, knocking him from his feet.

Ro was there in an instant, holding his long rifle just like the weapon that the other alien had and swinging it round in a blow aimed at the other alien's head that it barely ducked in time. It struck back, and now they were fighting in earnest. They swung their weapons like quarterstaffs, the weapons rattling against one another in a blistering display of blow and counter blow. Ro struck the Purest in the chest with the butt of his gun, knocking it back, but it countered with a low sweep that Ro had to leap to avoid. As he did so, the other alien smashed into him with a shoulder, knocking him back, then smashed the rifle out of his hands.

Kevin picked up his gun, firing straight at the Purest, but the golden armor seemed to deflect most of the shots. Ro stepped into that opening, twisting inside his opponent's guard and snatching the staff weapon from it, spinning and bringing an end full of crackling energy to bear.

The Purest fell, twitching.

Around Kevin, he could only see dead aliens, either blasted apart by General s'Lara's grenade or shot down in the brief fight that had followed. He dared to risk breathing a sigh of relief.

"Inside," General s'Lara said. "I've been coordinating by AI, but we've reached the point where we need to actually *talk* to the others."

The control room beyond the doors looked a lot like the other rooms of the complex, with screens for walls and a surprisingly soothing, soft environment. Kevin had been expecting large sets of controls, perhaps with joysticks to control weapons. Instead, at least a dozen important-looking Ilari just stood there, looking at the screens and occasionally discussing things with one another.

The screens held a lot more. Some of them held images of the fighting, while another had a plan of the complex with blue and red dots moving on it, probably designed to represent the Ilari and their enemies. Some held streams of numbers and data, and Kevin found that if he concentrated, he could make a kind of sense of it. Some of it seemed to be running simulations of different options for the battle, while other strands seemed to be intercepted communications, the sheer complexity of the Hive's connections too much to be presented any other way.

"What's the current situation?" General s'Lara asked.

One of the others turned to her. "The current situation is that we are in a lot of trouble, General. Hive craft are descending faster than we can pick them off with the energy cannons. Hive creatures are at the level of the forest floor, and many are attacking the trees themselves."

Something about the way he said that made it sound like a kind of sacrilege. After all the effort the Ilari had put into fitting into the environment of the world, maybe it was in a way.

"Numbers in the tree base?" General s'Lara asked.

"So far we have been able to hold them, but look for yourself." The man gestured to the screens, and on them, Kevin saw fight after fight between Ilari forces and those of the Hive. The friendly aliens fought with a perfect balance of precision and emotion, and Kevin saw them shoot down enemy after enemy. There always seemed to be another ready to step into the breach, though, and now Kevin could see the blue-skinned aliens falling, one by one. He saw a man brought down by energy blasts, and a woman ripped apart by one of the Hive's creatures. He saw an entire section of tree give way to fire from a squadron of fighter craft, and felt the rumble as more of the Hive blasted their way into the base.

It seemed so remote on the screens, but even so, Kevin could feel the horror of it. Those were *people* dying out there. Worse, every Ilari death, no matter how hard fought, was another step closer for the Hive.

"We need projections that will work," General s'Lara said, and then got the faraway look she had when she was talking to her AI.

As he had in the corridor, Kevin saw the flicker of different potential plans. Judging by the general's expression, none of them was what she was looking for.

"What's the problem?" Kevin asked.

"The problem is what it always is with the Hive: there are too many of them. Of all the ones we have killed today, only one will count to its members, and that is the gold-armored one in the hallway."

"When you say that there are too many…" Chloe began.

"I mean that there are more than we could ever hope to defeat," General s'Lara replied. "We have run simulation after simulation, but none of them… none of them offers a chance for us to survive. I'm sorry."

Kevin looked up at the screens again. On them, he saw death and destruction. He saw the Ilari being slowly overwhelmed by the weight of numbers. Worse, he could hear sounds from outside the room now: the tramp of feet and pincers, clawed legs and spines.

The Hive were coming for them there, in the control room.

CHAPTER SEVEN

There were too many aliens. Kevin could feel the fear rising in the room, because this wasn't the Hive, and the aliens there could feel the certainty of their deaths just as much as he could. Having AIs didn't make them any less afraid, or any more able to accept what was coming. Kevin could see red dots starting to fill the screen with the schematic for the building, while the ones showing images of the fighting showed death after death.

"There are too many of them," General s'Lara said, and Kevin could guess how serious things must have to be for the general to admit that. "I can't see a way for people to evacuate, or where we could go if we did."

Kevin knew what she was saying: they were all going to die there. He could feel the fear building up in him at that thought. The Ilari had only just cured him, and now he was going to be killed along with everyone else. Chloe, Ro, and the others were going to die; *were* dying, if the screens around Kevin were to be believed.

He stared at them for second after second, seeing the damage the Hive's forces was doing. In the battles in the sky, he could see their ships overwhelming the Ilari forces whenever they came up into clear air, and they were *forcing* them up into open space by firing at the trees below, setting them alight and burning them away.

The images from the inside were just as bad. Kevin could see the Ilari fighting bravely, combining their intuition and emotion with the logic and planning of their AIs to bring down enemy after enemy. Even so, it wasn't enough. There were always more, and the Hive's soldiers were willing to charge forward even if it meant their deaths. Their Purest commanders simply didn't care what happened to their troops, and since the one they'd already killed had been the only one on the ground so far…

"I have an idea," Kevin said, hoping that the thought that he'd just had would make sense.

"An idea?" one of the Ilari said. "Do you think there's any idea you could have that our AIs wouldn't have already put through a simulation?"

General s'Lara waved that away. "The whole *point* of what we are is the combination of living inspiration with the abilities of our AIs. If Kevin says he has an idea, we'll hear him out. What do you have in mind, Kevin? At this stage, I'm open to any ideas that we can get."

"We pretend to be the Purest," Kevin said. "We give them orders to… I don't know, pull back, or go the wrong places, stuff like that."

General s'Lara shook her head. "We've considered that possibility, but our AIs can't crack their communication codes. We would need a Purest's communicators to make it work, and direct access to the Hive is—"

"I can talk to them," Kevin said. "And we *have* a Purest, just outside this room."

"They have cut my connection to the Hive," Ro said, "but I may be able to do something, too."

"I need you to tell us where the communicators are," General s'Lara said, and for the first moment since the battle had begun, Kevin could see a glimmer of hope in her.

"Most are implanted, but for a battle like this, some would be a part of the war helm."

They knew what they needed, at least, now.

"Please," Kevin said. "It has to be worth a try."

General s'Lara considered for a moment, and again, Kevin had the sense of scenarios being played out in front of her. She nodded. "It's the best we have. It's a chance."

Kevin didn't want to ask how *much* of a chance. There were moments when calculating things precisely didn't help. That didn't matter right then anyway. They had to try this.

"Get ready," General s'Lara said, taking up a position by the doors to the control room. "Kevin, I want you to grab the helmet. You're the best choice for the job."

Kevin didn't ask why. He could already guess it: because all the others were seasoned warriors, and they would be needed to bring down as many of the Hive as possible.

"Everyone else, keep the enemy off him until we can get back inside."

She readied a gun and then nodded.

"On my count: three, two, one, *go!*"

The doors slid open, and ahead, Kevin saw a large group of the Hive's creatures, all pushing forward to try to get to the doorway. It took everything he had to bring himself to run forward, heading toward them and trusting that the others would be able to protect him. He did it, though, throwing himself out through the door, head down, eyes fixed on the helmet.

Energy fire burst all around him, flashing from his side to the aliens, and from them toward him. Flares of it burst off his shields, and Kevin tried to keep low, dodging and moving to try to avoid the worst of it.

General s'Lara and the others fired around him, hitting alien after alien, the energy of their attacks tearing them away from Kevin's path even when it didn't kill them outright. He kept his eyes on the fallen figure of the Purest ahead of him, the golden armor like a beacon amid the violence and the chaos of the fight.

"Die!" a black-armored creature yelled at him in a language that only Kevin's ability could translate, before swinging a blade of some matte-black, sharpened substance at him. Kevin ducked, and then saw Chloe leap into the fight beside him. Her shock stick came forward, held like a fencer's weapon, clashing against the blade again and again before darting through to catch the creature and send it flying back through the force of the energy it contained.

"Keep going!" Chloe yelled to him, and Kevin nodded before forcing his way forward.

He made it to the fallen figure of the Purest, holding back his disgust and trying to pull away the creature's golden helmet. It wouldn't budge, though, stuck in place no matter how Kevin yanked at it.

"You have to release it correctly," Ro said, rushing into place beside Kevin. "Here, let me."

The alien placed his fingers in what seemed like a carefully chosen pattern around the edge of the helmet, pressing them in. There was a hiss of escaping air, and the helmet gave way to reveal the coldly staring face of one of the Purest, frozen in death.

"This was Purest Kalix," Ro said. "He always sought the greatest role in things, so that—"

Ro cried out as a flash of energy hit him, and he tumbled to the ground, clutching his side. The golden helmet clattered from his hands, rattling on the floor as it spun there.

"Go," he yelled to Kevin. "Take the helmet. All of our lives depend on it."

Kevin grabbed the helmet, stuffing it under one arm like a football. He glanced back to see Chloe helping Ro up, while energy bolts flashed around him, cutting down more of the creatures in the hallway. The three of them ran for the doors, while the Ilari kept up their cascade of covering fire. Kevin hurried through the open doorway, throwing himself to one side as more shots came from the Hive's creatures. Chloe and Ro quickly followed, and the Ilari pulled back through the doors, sealing them shut once more.

"Are you all right?" Kevin asked Ro.

"There is no time," Ro said. "Focus on the helmet. I am cut off from the Hive. Only you can do this, Kevin. Put it on."

Kevin lifted the helmet. The interior seemed sculpted to its former owner, but Kevin lowered it down, the golden metal shielding his face from the outside world. A screen flickered into activity as Kevin put it on, showing the room around him, so that it seemed as though he could see in all directions at once.

"Now what?" Kevin asked.

"Touch here," Ro said, directing Kevin's hand. "That will activate the helmet's communications, fed into the Hive."

Kevin reached up to touch it, and as he did so, he could feel the nerves building within him. It wasn't just that so much rested on him being able to do this; it was fear of what might happen when he did. He'd been connected to the Hive before, and it had wiped away all sense of who he was. Kevin just hoped that this less complete connection would keep enough distance from the Hive that he could do what he needed to do. He didn't want to have to fight his way free of its grasp again.

He touched the helmet in the right spot, and for an instant, the inside of it filled with such a jumble of information that even his brain struggled to translate it all. Kevin knew then that this was what the communications of the Hive looked like from the outside. They didn't look beautiful from this angle, just the work of the endless implants and nanobots and more that connected the creatures they trapped.

Then his altered brain started to translate it, and Kevin found that he could access all of it easily.

It wasn't like being a true part of the Hive again. There was none of the overwhelming beauty of it all, or the sense of being a part of something much larger than he was. Kevin was still an outsider looking in, but he *could* look in, and he could see the orders and the counter orders of the various sectors of the Hive, the receiving minds of the soldiers and the drones, the complex living webs that made up its attack forces.

"If I just tell them to stop, they'll know that something is wrong," Kevin said, knowing that there would only be so much he could do without the Hive finding out and just ignoring anything that came from this helmet.

"Then talk to small groups of them," General s'Lara said. "Give them orders. Remember that they think you're one of the Purest."

Kevin nodded; that made sense. Being Purest meant not being questioned by anyone who wasn't. He didn't need to talk to the whole Hive, just to enough of the creatures that mattered. He moved in front of the wall of screens, trying to make sense of it all and work out which foes there connected with which minds in the vast communications web of the Hive. He spotted a group of ship pilots.

"Go low, into the trees," he commanded them. "The Ilari are warming up far more dangerous cannons, trying to draw us all out. Engage on their level."

He expected some argument there, or some challenge to the obvious lie, but instead, all that came back was a chorus of assent. On the screen, Kevin saw groups of enemy fighters breaking off from their strafing attacks in the clouds to dive into the trees, where he hoped the Ilari's greater skills might give them more of an advantage.

He saw a space where a small group of Ilari fighters was cut off, surrounded by the beasts and modified soldiers of the Hive's forces. Kevin looked at the base plans, working out where they were, and then looked into the Hive's communications, trying to work out which creatures they were.

"You are needed elsewhere," he commanded them. "Abandon all tasks at once, and proceed along the northwest corridor."

"Why that corridor?" Ro asked.

Chloe seemed to get it, though, jabbing a finger at the screen. "Because that one has more turrets."

On the screen, Kevin saw the creatures abandon their attack on the Ilari, moving off in the direction that he'd ordered. He saw the image shift to show the corridor, a dozen energy turrets opening up in concert. He'd done that, and he found himself caught between pride and shame. These creatures had to be fought, because they were the Hive's, but he knew that they had no real choice.

"Focus on all the people you're saving," Chloe said, obviously getting it.

Kevin took a breath.

"What next?" he asked General s'Lara.

"Calculating it now," she replied, and then pointed to a section of the outside world. "They have forces gathering here. Split them here, and here." She jabbed her finger at two more places. "That will make them small enough to pick off."

Kevin did it, sending the controlled creatures in directions where they wouldn't be able to hurt the Ilari forces. Again and again, he gave orders, feeling as though he was in a game of some kind, giving instructions and then watching the results on the screens. Every instruction he gave saved Ilari lives. Every instruction weakened the Hive's forces, and Kevin knew that there was still more that he could do.

"You fools!" he sent, to the creatures piloting ships, and weapons, and tank-like things, doing his best impersonation of one of the Purest. He could remember their arrogance and their certainty, at least. "You are failing the Hive. I demand direct control at once."

The influx of data was so great that Kevin swayed on his feet, but he wasn't weakened by his illness anymore. He wasn't going to collapse just because of the effort of everything that he needed to translate. He was strong enough now to do this, and to *keep* doing this. The helmet he wore gave him views from a thousand weapons platforms at once, and it might have been too many to keep track of if he wanted to make them fight more effectively, but Kevin didn't want to do anything like that. Instead, he reached out a hand to General s'Lara.

"If there's any way for your AI to connect to me and make use of this, do it now," he said.

He felt General s'Lara's hands upon him then, and something sharp jabbed into his neck. Kevin felt the sheer weight of information flowing through him in that moment, and he was the conduit for it, the point of connection. All he had to do was hold it in place.

He could hold. He had to. He was the only way that the Ilari could access any of this, and he was stronger now. There were none of the limits that there had been before.

Kevin stood there, holding together the two impossible to connect elements by sheer willpower, forcing his brain to pass on the complex instructions the AI sent, translating them as they came to him. He couldn't look at the screens now, but he could feel what was happening through his connection to the Hive's vehicles. He could feel the moment when the AI set them against one another, and they obeyed without question.

Kevin saw ships plunge downward, crashing into the ground and sending flames lancing up into the sky. He saw others turn their weapons on the ships around them, energy beams and gravity weapons ripping into one another, sending fragments of them cascading to the ground like rain.

He sent others on predetermined flightpaths, right into the crosshairs of Ilarian energy cannons. Kevin could feel the effort of translating so much, so quickly, taking control of so many of the enemy's forces, but now his body felt able to withstand that effort, keeping going as the Hive's forces started to destroy one another.

Kevin felt the Hive struggling to regain control, but by then, it didn't seem to matter anymore. So many of the Hive's ships were engaged in battle with one another by that point that the Ilari could easily strike at the rest, flitting between them and firing, bringing down enemy after enemy.

"We're winning," Chloe said. "We're actually *winning*."

Kevin felt the moment when the Hive cut the connection to the helmet he was wearing. It was too late though. He could see the enemy ships falling on the screens around him, while the Ilari cut through the ones who had landed easily now that he had been able to divide them up.

On one of the screens, he saw the air start to shimmer around the world ship hanging above the planet, twisting so that the stars beyond it seemed to shift positions as its gravity fields started to work. Kevin saw ships heading for it, rushing back with all the speed that they had cascaded down toward the surface. He saw them pull back into it, and the space around it twist even more, bending as though some giant hand was twisting and tearing at it.

The world ship vanished, its shadow disappearing from the sky as suddenly as it had come. It left behind emptiness, and silence, and an aching feeling that something impossible to understand had just happened.

A cheer broke out around the control room. Chloe threw her arms around him, while the Ilari seemed to be celebrating as they realized that they had survived everything that had just happened.

"We did it," Kevin said. "We've *won*."

General s'Lara, though, looked grave. "Not yet."

CHAPTER EIGHT

Around Kevin, the Ilari were picking up damaged equipment, while on the screens, he could see others tending to the injured, yet he couldn't focus on any of that. He was too busy staring at General s'Lara.

"What do you mean, this isn't over?" he asked. He felt almost… cheated. After all they'd done, how could the general say that? They'd won. They'd driven off the Hive. He was even cured. This *had* to be over now, didn't it?

"The Hive would not retreat just because they were losing soldiers," General s'Lara said. "They do not *care* about the creatures they lose. They do not feel fear. Kevin, you have felt what it was like. Would you have retreated when you were one of them?"

Kevin thought back to his brief time as a member of the Hive. General s'Lara was right; he hadn't known any fear beyond that of disappointing the Hive as a whole. If more of the Purest had been under threat, then they might have had a reason to pull back, but there hadn't been any others that he could see, only the one who had been so eager to be the one to win the fight that it had killed him. Even if the Purest had been in danger, any withdrawal would have only been temporary, while they worked out another way to strike.

That was what this had to be; it was the only thing that made any kind of sense. They would only pull back if they saw a more advantageous move to make on another part of the great board that was the galaxy. The same minds that had tricked Kevin and the world into exposing Earth to the vapor wouldn't just run when they could think of another way to strike out.

"It's true," Ro said. "The Hive won't stop so easily."

"But it's *done*," Chloe insisted, obviously not wanting to believe it. "We won."

Kevin had to shake his head then. "I'm sorry, Chloe. I think General s'Lara is right. I think they're just trying to attack another way."

He heard Chloe sigh. "I know. I just… I *want* it to be over." She waved her transformed arm. "All of it, all of this, and it still isn't done."

Kevin put an arm around her for comfort. "I know, and we will find a way to finish it."

Chloe turned toward him, and for a moment, it looked as though she might kiss him. Then she shook her head slightly, obviously remembering the conversation they'd had just before the Hive attacked. They both knew that Luna was the one Kevin loved. He just hated the thought that he might have hurt Chloe along the way.

"Why do we have to do anything?" one of the Ilari said. "We've driven them off. We've lost worlds to them. We've fought so many times. Our people have died and died for this moment. My AI says that at a maximum, this buys us a month in which to recover."

"And what happens after that?" General s'Lara asked.

"We can defend this place. With time to construct true shields—"

"The Hive will find a way around them," Kevin said. "They stole me away just to get around your others. What else might they do?"

"We will have time to deal with it, whatever it is," the Ilarian said. "We will have time to work out how to defeat them."

"And what else will they do with that time?" Chloe demanded. "How many years have the Hive been traveling everywhere, destroying whatever they found?"

"Centuries," General s'Lara said. "Too long."

"And in all that time, you never did anything about them?" Chloe said. "You sat behind your shields and you hoped that they would go away. You left evil out there, and now that you've managed to drive it off from your world, you're going to hide again and hope that the Hive goes away, no matter who it hurts."

"We've done our *part*," another of the Ilari said.

Kevin could understand that feeling. He'd had it, far too many times.

"A part of me wishes that I wasn't special," he said. "I think about everything that's happened, and I think 'why me?' I think about all the pain that I've been through, and everything that I've had to do. I've been across the world, and across the universe. I've seen people I care about hurt, and worse. A part of me wishes that I could just give up and stop this… but then, who will the Hive hurt next? I'll feel responsible for that. Won't you, when you're the ones who might have the power to stop them?"

"Stop them?" the Ilarian shot back, taking an angry step forward. "We've barely *survived* them."

General s'Lara stepped in between them, holding out her hands to keep them apart. "Stop this. This is not the moment for us to argue. There is too much rebuilding to do, and I want to know how much danger we are in, as well. At the very least, we should try to work out where the Hive is, and what they plan on doing next."

Kevin nodded. Whatever the Hive was doing, he wanted to know. They could be constructing a weapon, or building another army. They could be getting ready for their next attack even now, trying to catch the Ilari by surprise.

"*Can* we find out?" he asked. "The Hive's world ship vanished."

"It's a world," General s'Lara said. "Our sensors will be able to track it, even folding space like that. From there, the AIs will be able to extrapolate its path, and the likely resources the Hive are trying to harvest."

Of course the Hive would be looking for resources. Kevin had known that same need when he was a part of it, trying to find more and more to ensure its survival, and its eventual perfection. A defeat like this would only push that need further. It would want the resources it required to come back and finish this task.

"And if you establish what they seek," Ro guessed, "it may be possible to work out what their plan is."

"Exactly," General s'Lara said. She moved to a section of the wall that was displaying sensor readings around the planet. As she approached, the wall shifted, showing maps of what Kevin guessed was the star system, then the surrounding galaxy.

For a moment, it seemed blank, but then he saw a line of red dots where the Hive's world ship had passed. An even more faint line tracked ahead of it, and Kevin guessed that was the path General s'Lara's AI was predicting for it. The path shifted slightly from moment to moment, but Kevin could already see the direction that it was heading in. It took him a moment or two to recognize the spot it was passing through.

"Earth," he said. "The Hive ship is heading back to Earth."

The full horror of that thought made his blood run cold. He had thought that the Earth would at least be safe now that the world ship had gone with him and Chloe on it, but now...

"Why are they going back?" Chloe asked. "Are they just giving up on here and going back to their last target?"

Kevin couldn't imagine the Hive doing anything so simple. Nor, it seemed, could General s'Lara.

"I don't think that it's as straightforward as that," she said. "There's a reason why they targeted Earth, and it wasn't just that it was there. There was always something on it that they wanted, or they would have picked a different world, a different species. The question is what." She paused for a moment, then looked over at Ro. "Do you know anything about why they targeted Earth? What did they *want*?"

Kevin watched Ro try to think. He understood how difficult it was being cut off from the Hive. It wasn't as though all of its information was at Ro's fingertips anymore, or like any member of it would have thought to pull out all the information they wanted into their own head. Why do so, when they could just reach into the mind of another creature and find it?

"Try to think, Ro," he said. "There must be some reason."

"Remember when we met the Survivors?" Chloe said. "Remember the quarry where they forced people to work, and tested them?"

Kevin nodded, thinking about it. At the time, they'd assumed that it was all part of the process of stripping Earth of all its resources, or maybe some vile plan to work out who the strongest people were so that they could take only those for their ship. Now, he found himself wondering exactly what they had been mining, and why.

"They were mining something," Kevin said. "They were searching for something specific."

Ro thought some more before nodding.

"There was a material," he said. "The others seemed to think that it could be a danger to us, but also a potential weapon. That it could magnify the vibrational frequencies of energy put into it. We hoped to use it in weapons that might rip through Ilarian shields. It was only when we found Kevin that we decided to use him instead."

"You said it was a danger to the Hive?" General s'Lara said.

Ro shrugged.

"You have to understand that I do not know all of it," the alien said. "I believe that part of the answer lies in the way the Hive connects to others; in the nanites we use to achieve that connection. I think the idea is that the specific vibrational properties of that substance, if tuned correctly…"

"…might undo the effects of the vapor?" Kevin guessed, barely able to believe that thought. It fit with what he knew of the Hive, though, and the way that it worked.

"It's a cure," Chloe said, looking astonished. "All this time, and a cure was sitting on Earth."

Kevin's heart leapt at that thought, because it meant that there might be a way to get things back to how they had been. They could cure the whole of humanity, they could cure his mother…

…They could cure Luna.

As huge as that was, though, it was only a part of the whole. Kevin could see how much more there was to it.

"It's a weapon against the Hive," he said. "It can't kill them, but it can tear apart their connection; the thing that *makes* them the Hive. Without it, at best, it's just the Purest we would be fighting. Maybe not even them."

That thought felt like a ray of hope shining through the dark clouds that had engulfed everything since the beginning of this. Then General s'Lara spoke again.

"This substance is on Earth, and the Hive are heading there for it, ready to take or destroy it."

Kevin thought about the mines, and all the work that the Hive had put in, trying to steal from the planet. He thought about the weapon that he had seen used against the Ilari planet, and the danger that it represented.

"They're going to take as much of the material for themselves as they can," he guessed, "then destroy Earth so that no one else can find it."

"And to fuel their endless quest for resources," Ro agreed and then nodded. "I believe so, yes."

"But we still have a chance!" Chloe insisted, sounding unwilling to give up on the idea. "If there's something on Earth that can stop them… don't *all* of you want that?"

Kevin nodded, looking around the room at the others there, looking at the ones who had voiced their concerns in particular. He could see the excitement on a lot of the faces, in spite of their objections before. Only one of them spoke up against it now, looking gravely concerned.

"There's still the problem that the Hive has a head start on us," he said, "and that gravity technology of theirs lets them move far faster than any of our current ships. We can't hope to get there before them."

"It will take them time to act to use their weapon," General s'Lara said. "As Ro here has pointed out, such a weapon requires time to build up its charge."

"Even so, we might be better off taking the time to find another world to run to. One we can defend. We can't make it to Earth in time to stop this."

General s'Lara cocked her head to one side. "We can if we use the *Dart*."

A low rumble of mutters went around the room. From it, Kevin got the impression that the general might have hit on an option that could work. Even so, people didn't seem happy with the idea.

"What's the *Dart*?" Kevin asked.

"It's suicide, is what it is," the Ilari who had spoken said. "You know that it isn't ready yet, and—"

"The *Dart* is an experimental ship," General s'Lara said, cutting the man off before he could finish. "It is faster than anything else in our fleet. It is unfinished yet, because there have been some… teething troubles."

"People died!" the Ilari who had spoken insisted.

"And many more people will die if we do not get to the Earth in time." General s'Lara beckoned, and Kevin followed along with the others as she led the way through the corridors of the tree base.

The route was a long one, and Kevin found it hard to keep track of exactly where they were going, but he had the general impression that they were heading downward, little by little. They kept heading down, and now they came out through large, metallic doors onto a forest floor littered with the wreckage of the battle. Kevin saw Ilari moving here and there, clearing away the scrap, and pulling bodies from the remains of ships. Kevin was surprised to see some of them helping creatures that obviously belonged to the Hive, but he guessed that he shouldn't have been; the Ilari practiced peace, even when it came to their defeated enemies.

"This way," General s'Lara said, leading the way through all of it. People called out to her and she saluted some of them, but she kept going even though Kevin had the feeling that she wanted to stop and talk.

"Do you think this *Dart* thing will work?" Kevin asked. "Some of the people back there didn't sound so certain."

General s'Lara looked back at him. "I hope so. Here."

A section of the forest floor moved aside, and Kevin knew it had to be in response to a signal from her AI. A ramp led down, and again, the general led the way along it. There were empty rooms there, with what looked like half-finished projects of all kinds: everything from weapons and shields to more peaceful things; the kind of things a world that wasn't at war might need to reshape trees, or grow better food, or heal people.

A hangar space sat beyond them, and in it…

Kevin could barely believe the ship that sat there, pointed up toward the sky like its namesake. The *Dart* was sleek and white, bulbous at one end, with fins that seemed to be covered in panels that flickered with shields. The whole thing looked as though it was ready to thrust up into space, being thrown between one world and the next.

"Our scientists assure us that it will cut through the space between this reality and others," the general said. "The speeds it will achieve are far beyond those of even our fastest ships at the moment."

Speed was important. Speed was what would get them to Earth in time to do something. There was at least one other thing that they needed to think about, though.

"How dangerous is it?" Kevin asked.

General s'Lara spread her hands. "It is untested technology, at least in this final form. Cutting through dimensions like this is potentially risky."

On another day, that might even have mattered. With the Earth at risk, though, Kevin knew that they were going to have to do this, no matter how bad it was.

"I'll go," Kevin said.

General s'Lara nodded. "As will I, and anyone else of my people who will come. The *Dart* is not large, but it will hold some of us; the best warriors we have left. The rest of our fleet will follow, and I hope that it will arrive in time."

"The rest?" one of the others asked. "You're sending *all* the fleet? What if the Hive comes back?"

"Then this world is lost," General s'Lara said, so simply that Kevin could feel the shockwaves that sent through the room. His ability gave him the impression of AIs furiously debating with one another, not even beginning to agree.

"You're really sending all of them?" Kevin asked. He hadn't thought that the general would do that.

General s'Lara nodded. "I believe that this is the best chance we have, Kevin. This will be the last battle of this war. If we do not win it, then everything is lost."

Kevin swallowed, looking up at the *Dart*. This was it.

"Then we have to win."

CHAPTER NINE

Luna tried not to show how tired she was as she worked with the Survivors to salvage what equipment they could from the factory. She needed them to see that she was fine, and that the cure had worked perfectly. The peace between them and the soldiers who had held it still felt too fragile, too much like it might fall apart if she showed the least sign of turning back.

Not that she would. She was cured for good this time; she could feel it.

"Exactly how many weapons do you have?" Luna asked Captain Harris. The man seemed friendlier than he had, but even so kept a wary distance from her, as if she might try to strike at him at any moment.

"Enough to win against gangs and groups of those things. Not enough to win an entire war, if that's what you're thinking."

"They aren't things," Luna corrected him. "There are people still trapped in each and every one of the controlled. We can save them, and build our army at the same time."

"If you say so," Captain Harris said, with surprising deference this time. Then again, Luna was the girl they had seen come back. Even though more than half of the others there had once been controlled, she was the one who had been cured most obviously, and her actions in the fight back at the university had cured so many others too.

"I do say so," Luna said. "Every person we shoot is a win for the aliens, while every one we turn back is a loss for them. We have a cure now. We can do this."

Captain Harris nodded, and Luna held back her dislike of the man. She reminded herself that he was just trying to do his best to protect the people who followed him. Luna could feel the same pressure to look after people inside of her, except that, for her, it was the entire world she wanted to protect.

"I want you to give weapons to as many people who know how to use them as possible," Luna said. "I want you to train people to use them well, so that when we're fighting the *actual* aliens, we have a chance."

"Yes, ma'am," he said, and Luna laughed at that.

"Did you just call me ma'am?" She wasn't old enough to be a ma'am. She didn't feel authoritative enough, either, although people

59

seemed to be treating her as though she was. Luna's army, she could hear them starting to call themselves, when all she'd done… well, she guessed she'd done a few things, between changing most of them back, being the first to be cured their new way and the rest, but it still felt weird that she seemed to be in charge.

"I have to go talk to the others," she said. "We need to work things out. Can you get started with the weapons?"

"Yes m… Luna," Captain Harris said. He still saluted.

Luna went down through the factory, toward the spot where Ignatius and Barnaby were still working with the machinery that had crafted the cure for her, Ignatius doing it on makeshift crutches now, his leg wrapped in bandages that looked as though they had come from a particularly ancient first aid kit. Leon was there, talking to them as they started to make plans, and Luna headed toward them.

Cub was there, moving into sight almost as soon as she went across, stepping out into her path from a group of the Survivors. If Luna had spotted him earlier, she might have been able to pick a different route, but now she couldn't turn away without it looking as though she was avoiding him. Luna wouldn't let him think that she was doing that, if only because he didn't deserve to make her feel like that.

"Luna, wait," he said.

The worst part, the very worst, was that he still looked good to her. He still had the dangerous good looks that had made him so exciting to be around, had made Luna's heart flutter a little whenever he got close. She still felt a kind of echo of it now, but it was just her brain being stupid, and she overruled it.

"What do you want, Cub?" she asked.

"I want to talk," he said. "Please."

A part of Luna wanted to walk away anyway, wanted to make an excuse and just keep walking toward the others, but that felt too much like running away. She looked at Cub instead, waiting for him to say whatever he had to say so that she could get this over with.

"Well?" she asked.

"Luna, don't be like this," Cub said. "I… you know how I feel about you."

"I got a pretty good idea when you pointed a gun at me," Luna said, unable to keep the hurt out of her voice. That was the kind of betrayal that didn't go away easily, no matter what someone said afterward.

Cub stepped back like she'd slapped him. A part of Luna kind of wished she had.

"You know why I did that," he said. "I couldn't stand to see you there like that. I thought that you were lost."

"You *know* it doesn't work like that," Luna said. "You *knew* that I would still be in there, because you've *been there.*"

"I've been there," Cub agreed, "and I know that I wouldn't want to be like that. I would want you to shoot me if it came to it. I wouldn't want to be stuck like that."

Luna could kind of understand that. She even knew why. She had been there when Cub had been forced to kill his own father to protect her and the others. She knew *why* Cub had wanted to kill her. She just couldn't believe that he'd actually tried to do it.

"Just so we're clear," Luna said. "You know, in case it ever comes up again. I don't want you to shoot me."

"Luna—" Cub began, but Luna cut him off.

"It isn't just that, Cub," she said, although she had to admit that it was a pretty big piece of it. "When I was transforming, I had to try to cling to something to keep a sense of myself. I picked Kevin."

Luna could picture Kevin even now as he had been in her mind's eye. She found that thoughts of him came so easily it was hard to concentrate on Cub. She tried to focus on him, but even so, she found herself thinking about how Kevin would have given everything to try to save her. He wouldn't have even considered shooting her. He wouldn't have given up like that.

"Kevin?" Cub said. Luna could hear the hurt there, then the harshness. "He's gone, Luna."

Luna shook her head. She wasn't going to let Cub take him from her like that. "He'll find a way to get back. We're going to win this."

She wasn't going to give up. She was going to make sure they got through this.

"It was always about Kevin, wasn't it?" Cub demanded, and now there was something unpleasant in his voice. "I never really had a chance, did I? What do I have to do?"

Luna stepped past him. "There's nothing. I'm sorry."

She kept going, so that Cub wouldn't see the tears at the corners of her eyes. It wasn't Cub that she wanted, but it still hurt to actually say it. Luna had to force herself to keep going, walking over to Barnaby, Leon, and Ignatius, knowing that if she was talking to them, Cub wouldn't be able to follow and demand answers.

Besides, they needed to keep planning. They needed to find a way to take back the world. They needed to *fight.*

"How much of the cure do you have now?" Luna asked.

"Not enough to change the whole world," Leon said. "We don't have enough materials to change more than a few hundred more of the controlled."

It wasn't enough. A few hundred was nothing against the numbers of those the Hive had changed. They needed enough of the cure for everyone, and they needed a way to deliver it. To do that, they needed to find more of the mineral, and Luna wasn't sure where they would be able to get it when the sample they had was one that had come from a meteorite.

Barnaby didn't seem perturbed by any of this. Instead, he seemed to be drawing designs for things that looked like weapons.

"What are you drawing?" Luna asked.

"I'm trying to improve the ways we have to deliver the cure," Barnaby said. "I mean… dart guns, obviously, but those can only change one person at a time back."

"Maybe some kind of gas grenade?" Luna suggested.

Barnaby nodded. "That could work. And also more gas guns like Ignatius's."

Leon didn't look happy though.

"Converting the controlled is one thing," he said. "We still need to find weapons that can defeat the aliens, or it won't make any difference."

Luna had been thinking about that. More than that, she'd been thinking about the battle back at the university. She could remember the moment when alien fighter ships had fired down at her with one of the meteorite shards, and the shockwave that had come from it had felt all encompassing.

"I think that the cure *is* the weapon," she said. "You saw how the shards changed the battle. They affected all of their creatures, not just the controlled people. Even their ships flew off. What if the people flying them are controlled too? What if we can use the cure as a weapon?"

"It will be hard to shoot ships with dart guns," Leon pointed out.

"But we know how the material reacts with the aliens' energy," Ignatius said. "If we had more of it…"

"We *don't* have more of it though," Leon said. "We need to find more, and we don't know where to look."

Luna had a thought then. "What about the quarry?"

"The quarry?" Barnaby repeated. From his haunted look, Luna guessed that he was thinking back to his time as a prisoner there. It had been where they'd first met him, and it had not looked like a place anyone would want to go back to.

"Think about it," Luna said. "Doesn't it make sense that if there were some kind of special material, the aliens would want to dig it up before anything else? Doesn't it make sense that they would be looking for it?"

The others paused. Gradually, one by one, they nodded.

"Think, Barnaby," Luna said. "You know what the mineral looks like now. Did you see anything like it?"

Barnaby was quiet. Then he nodded. "I... I think so. I remember carts of materials we couldn't identify. I think... some of them might have been similar."

"It sounds like our best shot," Luna said, although she found herself thinking back to all of the controlled who had been there in the quarry. If they were still there, this would be both difficult and dangerous.

"You want to go, don't you?" Leon asked.

Luna nodded. "If this turns out to be true, if we can get more of the cure, then we can win this. We can start to make weapons with it. We can beat the aliens by taking away the things that connect them together. Get people together. We need to be ready to fight."

She waited while the others started to make their preparations. Captain Harris was already handing out weapons, while Barnaby and Ignatius started to pass round the samples of the cure that they had. Luna took one of the syringes, feeling the weight of it in her hand.

"Just stab them anywhere, and it will work," Barnaby said. "Are you sure you don't want to stay behind though? You've only been turned back a little while."

Luna shook her head. "That's exactly why people need to see me doing this. They need to see that I am human again, and that we can win against the things the Hive tries to do to us. They'll follow me. I can't send them off to take this kind of risk without going myself. While we're gone, the two of you should keep working on ideas to use the cure. The energy blast we got in the battle changed so many people back, but it will be hard to repeat."

"I will try to think of something," Ignatius promised. "Good luck, Luna."

***

They made their way up toward the quarry, and it was a smaller group than Luna was getting used to marching with by now, because this group contained only clusters of those people they knew could fight. Leon stood at their head, while Luna traveled further back, surrounded by people who seemed determined to protect her. Even Cub was there, bringing up the rear and looking determined too, as if he might somehow be able to make Luna feel something if he could only prove himself.

Luna really hoped he wasn't thinking like that.

"Keep quiet and keep down," Luna said as they got closer. "There were a lot of the controlled here the last time."

She moved out of the main group of people, and she and Leon headed up one of the hills near the rim of the quarry, sneaking around to the spot where she, Chloe, and Kevin had looked out over it before.

Below, she saw controlled overseeing the mining operation, people working hard to dig out rocks with hand tools and cutters, never daring to slacken their pace for fear of being dragged away to be changed into one of the creatures themselves. Now that she knew what to look for, Luna was sure that some of them held the bluish sheen of the cure's minerals.

"Now we know why they force humans to do the mining in these places," Luna said. "We thought it was just about testing them, but what if it was because this is one place the controlled *can't* work? What if there's too much risk of them being changed back?"

That thought seemed to make sense. How frustrating would it be for the aliens that they couldn't just take what they wanted here? Wouldn't they try to force people to do what they wanted if they couldn't simply change them?

"How do we do this?" Leon asked.

Luna looked down again. She could see the controlled acting as guards there, and there were other creatures too now. Some wore black armor that made them look like knights, carrying rifle-like weapons.

"We need to start by targeting them," she said, pointing to the armored figures. She lifted her syringe. "We move in close and stab them, then..."

"Then *hope* that they're controlled too, and not just happy to do this?" Leon demanded, in a skeptical tone.

Luna knew he was right; they couldn't just ask people to take on so many of the aliens with no guarantee that it would work. That left only one option...

"Luna, wait!" Leon called out, as Luna ran down toward the quarry, keeping low and out of sight. She didn't wait for anyone else's permission, because she didn't need it. She *did* need to do this, because it was their best chance.

"What do you think you're doing?" Leon asked, as he caught up.

"Putting this to the test," Luna said. She tried to pick out the armored figure closest to the edge, looking for one she could get to without a dozen others spotting her.

"Luna!" Leon began, but Luna shushed him.

"They'll hear you," Luna said. She crept forward as she spotted a black-armored figure alone, trying to work out if there were any chinks in its metallic carapace. She thought she spotted grayish skin in the gap between the shoulder plates and the helmet. She took one careful step forward, then another, holding the syringe like a knife.

She really hoped this worked.

Luna put a hand on the alien's armored shoulder, then stabbed into the gap with the syringe, feeling the skin beneath break as it jabbed into the flesh below. Luna pressed the plunger down in one smooth movement, sending the cure pumping into the alien's body.

It spun and pushed her away, letting out a cry in an alien language that she couldn't begin to understand.

It had a gun in its hands whose barrel looked more like the half-open mouth of some deadly creature. Luna saw the glow of energy there, and she got ready to throw herself to the side, but she knew she wouldn't be fast enough. She was going to die.

Then the alien spun and fired at another of its black-armored brethren, the blast of energy bringing it down with its armor smoking. It fired again, and another of the aliens fell.

"So much for subtle," Leon said, moving up beside her. "We need to get back to the others. We need—"

Energy fire sent them both scampering for cover, ducking down behind a combination of bushes and dirt to try to shield themselves from the violence. Luna kept her head down, while energy flashed around her, and she knew that the aliens would be closing in, gaining ground on them second by second, until…

The others from her erstwhile army came thundering over the hill in one great horde, weapons firing as they came, trying to drive back the aliens.

"Cure the ones in black!" Luna yelled above the noise. "They can fight!"

She wasn't sure if the others had heard her at first, but then she saw them surging toward the armored figures. A dozen of her people swarmed one of them, holding it in place while another jabbed a syringe into it. The creature quickly rose, firing with its weapon at the others.

Luna waded into the fight, shoving another one which looked as though it was about to fire its rifle into the path of more of her people. They grabbed for it, holding it in place again while the cure did its work. Obviously, Ignatius had listened to her idea about grenades, or maybe he was just using some of his old, temporary cure, because she saw people throwing glass globes filled with mist.

That made it sound like a clean, careful fight, but there was still death; far too much death. Where the controlled got in close to her people, their strength let them break bones and toss bodies aside. The armored figures who had yet to be changed fired with their energy weapons, blasting people back wherever they struck. Her own people fired with rifles and pistols, bringing down one of the armored creatures, and far too many of the controlled. Luna could imagine Cub far too easily, firing along with the rest of them, killing as many as he could.

Slowly though, step by step, they cleared the quarry.

"Fight back!" Luna called to the human slaves still trapped there. "Help us and we can win this."

They struck out with the tools they had—picks and hammers and shovels. It wasn't much in the face of energy weapons or the great strength of the controlled, but it was something, and with the cure that Luna's forces had, it slowly started to prove enough. Luna charged into a fresh group of enemies, knocking one of them down with her weight so that her people could transform it.

Eventually, she looked around and there were no more enemies left, only people standing there staring at her.

"Lu-na, Lu-na, Lu-na!"

The chant started quietly, but slowly rose in volume, until it seemed that Luna was basking in a sea of sound.

"We've done it," she said to Leon. "We have the quarry. We can make more of the cure. We can *do* this."

They could do this. They could win this.

Luna was still thinking of that when she saw the shadow slip into place over the world. It was a shadow that was far too familiar. Even before she looked up, Luna knew what she would see. A part of her felt hopeful, because it meant the possibility that Kevin and Chloe might have returned, but far more of her felt apprehension.

The world ship was back.

CHAPTER TEN

Luna stood in the shadow of the world ship, pointedly not looking up at it, determined to look after her people regardless of its presence up there. She looked around at the small army that they'd gathered, still barely able to believe that so many people were looking to her for guidance.

"All right," she said. "We need to bring Barnaby and Ignatius here so that they can test the materials we've found and make sure they are actually something we can use. Captain Harris, I want you to help train the people the aliens enslaved, so that they have a chance when it comes to fighting back. You guys…" She looked across to the black-armored former soldiers of the aliens. "You probably can't understand a word I'm saying. I *really* wish Kevin were here right now."

She didn't just wish it because Kevin would be able to talk to the aliens directly, rather than making hand signals and hoping they understood. She wanted him there just so that he could *be* there, with her, while they started making preparations to save the world from the aliens hanging overhead.

Maybe he was here. Maybe he was up there somewhere, along with Chloe. Luna clung to that hope, even though, right then, there were far too many other things that pulled that hope away.

"We need people to continue to mine," Luna said. "I'm not going to make anybody do it, but if Barnaby and Ignatius confirm what that stuff is, then it might be our best chance to actually win this."

She saw people moving toward the tools they'd been using in the quarry before, hefting them in calloused hands and starting to work on the walls, starting to pull out more of the mineral. If they got enough of it, then maybe there would be a chance to change all of this. Maybe they would be able to cure everyone who needed the cure.

"We'll need other things to fight this," Leon said, coming up to Luna. He pointed up toward the world ship. "There's a whole world of aliens up there. We'll need more than just… well, more than *us* to fight them."

Luna nodded at that thought. They would need more than just the Survivors. They would need all the remaining people of Earth; everyone who could fight against the aliens, all at once. In the last

67

battle, there hadn't even *been* a real fight, because the aliens had taken over the world's people before they could fight back. What would happen if they could fight back? What would happen if they *did*?

"This time, we'll fight them," Luna said. "Leon, can you find a way to contact other groups?"

"Communications are still hit and miss," he said. "I can send out messages to other local groups, and I guess, for people further off…"

"Send messengers to them too," Luna said. "Tell them about the cure. Tell them how it can be a weapon, and how it reacts to the aliens' energy blasts. That news is the biggest weapon we have right now. We need them all to fight back at once, or there will be too many aliens."

Too many; a whole world's worth. Now, Luna allowed herself to look up, taking in the shape of the world ship. It hung there, rocky and waiting, ships already starting to come and go from it as it resumed squatting above the world like a toad.

For a moment, Luna paused, thinking about just how difficult this would be, but she forced herself to ignore that thought. This wasn't about things being difficult or easy; it was about the survival of humanity as a whole. If they didn't fight back, then who would?

"Any of you who don't have a job to do yet," she called out to the others there, "I want you to focus on finding food and shelter for everyone, or helping to scout, or anything else you can think of to do. A situation like this will need all of us working together. We all have to do our parts, and the world might depend on it."

She left them to get on with the many jobs involved, knowing that as soon as this started, there would be far too much for her to do. There was. It seemed that, almost as soon as people broke away from celebrating their victory, they started to run into problems with what came next. More than that, it seemed that every one of those problems required Luna's personal attention.

"Explain the problem to me," Luna said, as a group of people gesticulated and shouted, standing in front of the black-armored aliens who had come over to their side.

"They… they're the *enemy*," a woman there said. "They *enslaved* us, and now they're just standing around the mine with no payback for anything they did."

"They were just as enslaved as you were," Luna said. "You saw the way they fought for us the moment we gave them the cure? That's because the aliens were controlling them, the same way that they have been controlling people on Earth. Now leave them alone and let them help. There's a fight coming, and if they're prepared to help us, then we should be kinder to them than this."

The woman stepped back, and it was a strange feeling for Luna, having adults like this listening to her. They *did* listen, though, stepping back and getting on with the work of mining the mineral from the quarry's walls. Soon, it seemed that everyone was working toward some fragment of the greater whole that was the fight against the aliens' forces.

"I think… I think I've been able to set up a meeting with all the other nearby groups using shortwave," Leon said. "Some of them are pretty jumpy though. They think that it's some kind of trap. They want to meet out in the open and…"

"And you don't trust them either?" Luna guessed. She could understand that, she guessed. She'd seen firsthand that the end of the world as they knew it had brought out the worst in a lot of people.

"There's a lot that could go wrong," Leon said. "I'll go, and we'll take as many of the soldiers as we can. We'll make it into a show of strength."

Luna shook her head to that thought. "That's not how you get people to work with you," she said. "We'll take some people, but I'll go too, and I want us to bring at least one of the aliens with us. I want us to be able to show them that we can win this. I want us to give them hope."

Leon looked as though he might argue, but he didn't. That was almost as strange as the rest of it, because Luna was used to him being the leader, telling the Survivors what to do. Somewhere in all of this, it seemed that he'd come to respect her as much as the others had.

"All right," he said. "Get ready to leave and I'll get a few people to see if they can scavenge some bikes together."

***

Luna sat on her bike with Bobby the dog in its sidecar. Around her, a dozen other assorted vehicles made their way in formation, heading toward the open plaza where Leon had arranged the meeting. They'd managed to get one of the black-armored aliens onto the back of one of them, his weapon slung across his back, even though it didn't seem to understand where it was going.

Luna had brought a couple of other things too: a small bag of syringes filled with the cure, and a chunk of the mineral that formed its basis. She figured that, at the very least, she would be able to tell people how to cure the controlled for themselves.

The LA streets were still choked with the abandoned hulks of cars, but the bikes were able to pick their way between them. Bobby sat in the sidecar, his tongue lolling as they made their way toward the spot arranged for the meeting.

"You look a lot more carefree than I am," Luna told the dog. "But then, I guess you don't have to worry about what happens next."

There were so many questions going around in her mind as she approached the heart of the plaza. What if she'd misjudged this? She'd met enough of the gangs of this new world to know what it could be like, so what if these betrayed them? What if this turned out to be an ambush? What if they saw the alien Luna had brought with her, and lashed out? What if she just couldn't persuade them to take her seriously? What if the aliens learned where she was and attacked?

Despite all of those worries, Luna did what she knew she had to: she went to the center of the plaza and waited. And waited. She stood there by her borrowed bike, trying to look as non-threatening as possible, while she hoped that nobody watching had her in the crosshairs of some kind of weapon.

Gradually, people started to arrive. The first group came in on foot, sloping in with hoods up and weapons ready. The next group roared in on bikes that more than matched Luna's, circling the plaza once as if checking it for enemies before coming to a halt. More and more of them approached, spreading out in a rough semicircle while eyeing the others there warily.

"Who are you?" one of the hooded men demanded. "We thought it was Leon of the Survivors who called us here."

"Like he's some kind of leader to all of us," a man from another group said. "Instead, he sends some girl?"

Luna stepped forward. "Leon asked you all here because I asked him to. You've seen the world ship come back into the sky. The aliens are coming back, and we need to fight them."

"Fight them?" a tough-looking man in biker leathers said, derisively. "You've got one of them *with* you."

"We... served them," the black-armored figure said, and Luna spun toward him.

"You speak our language?" Luna said, as much in shock at that as any of the others must have been.

"I... am learning it," the creature said. "I am... Ka. We served... and Luna freed us... we will fight."

"How?" another of those there demanded. "We can't fight so many when they can just change us into things, or kill us with weapons we've never seen."

Luna was about to explain about the cure when a mixture of car horns and sirens started to sound from among the nearby buildings. Luna knew from the Survivors what that meant, even before the first of the controlled started to stalk from the buildings. They'd been found.

"Here they come," the man in the hood said. "Time to leave."

A part of Luna wanted to turn and run with them, because there were so many of them this time. Not as many as at the university, perhaps, and none of the larger, more deadly creatures the aliens had brought to the world, but there were still too many to fight head on with only a few rifles and pistols. They came out running in a single, living mass of controlled people, and now it seemed to Luna that even if she did turn the bike and flee, it wouldn't be enough.

Instead, she took out the lump of mineral that she had brought with her, weighing it in her hand. She turned to the alien in the black armor.

"How accurately can you shoot, Ka?" she asked, hoping that he would understand her intentions, even if he didn't get all of her words.

He considered the mineral shard, and then nodded.

Luna hefted it one more time and then threw it overhand, spearing it out toward the crowd of the controlled, sending it arcing just above them. For a moment, she thought that the alien beside her had misunderstood.

Then a bolt of energy flashed out from the energy rifle, crossing the space between it and the mineral shard in an instant. There was a brief ripple of resonance from the shard, then Luna threw herself flat as it exploded.

This explosion wasn't on the scale of the one that had spread out over the battlefield of the university. The shard wasn't big enough for that, or the energy the rifle put out wasn't enough. It was the same alien energy that the mineral had reacted to before, though, and it was enough to create a boom that made Luna wish she'd thought to clamp her hands over her ears before it could happen.

In its wake, the controlled who had been attacking lay on the floor, looking as though they had simply been flattened by the explosion. As they started to stand, though, Luna could hear them starting to talk to one another, see them looking around in confusion as they tried to make sense of what had just happened to them. They were human again, and free.

More than that, they were a symbol.

"It works," the man in the hood said, something like awe in his voice. "You have a cure."

"We have a *weapon*," Luna corrected him. "We can take the controlled away from them. We can show you how. We can give you a cure. We'll give you that whatever you want to do, but I'm asking you to help."

The hooded man considered for a moment, then nodded. "My people will be there."

"So will mine," another of the leaders there declared.

"And mine," a third said.

Luna beamed as they declared themselves a part of her growing army, but she only stood there as long as she had to in order to hear it. Her priorities were elsewhere. As soon as she could, Luna went across to the former controlled. They were the ones who needed her help most in that moment. They were the ones who would be shaken and afraid, not knowing what was happening.

"It's all right," she told them. "My name's Luna. I know what it's like. You felt like you were prisoners in your own bodies, and maybe you couldn't even remember what was happening."

"How do you know that?" a woman asked.

The answer to that was simple. "I've been controlled like you, but you're safe now. Come with me, and I'll lead you back to where it's safe."

She led them back, step by step, toward the quarry. Bobby walked by her side, the dog's weight reassuring next to her whenever he brushed against her.

"They'll be wondering where we are," Luna said to him, knowing that the Survivors would be expecting her to ride back, not walk, and *certainly* not walk with so many.

Bobby barked in response.

By the time they got back to the quarry, it was starting to get dark, and there were plenty of people watching with weapons. Luna could see Cub up there on the walls, but she ignored him. It was better than remembering the gun he'd pointed her way.

"You were gone a long time," Leon said as Luna approached.

She nodded. "I wanted to walk back with the others. Besides, I know you'll have been running things just fine."

Leon nodded. "That's… good to hear. We've been busy. I've sent out people to look for other mining operations; I figure that the aliens might have targeted other spots where they could find the mineral."

That was good thinking, and Luna found herself wishing that she'd thought of it.

"I also sent out messengers the way you wanted," Leon said. "I hope people across the world will know about the cure before long. But…"

"What?" Luna asked.

Leon shook his head. "It might not matter. There's something Barnaby and Ignatius worked out. Something bad. Come on. They can tell you."

He led the way through their new camp, to the spot where the two were working. Bobby followed her. To Luna's surprise, so did the alien, Ka. Barnaby and Ignatius seemed to be looking at a hastily written equation on a board.

"What is it?" Luna asked.

"We know that they've destroyed worlds before, right?" Ignatius said.

Luna nodded. Kevin had said it. Kevin had *seen* it.

"It seems to be drawing up some kind of energy," Barnaby said, nodding toward the world ship. "Slowly, but it's doing it. We're sure of it. Some of the aliens you 'saved' have talked about it."

"You think it's getting ready to destroy the Earth?" Luna said.

Barnaby nodded.

"How long do we have?" she asked.

"We've been trying to work that out," Ignatius said. "There are so many variables though. How much energy does it take to destroy a world? How fast can they draw it in? How much—"

"Thirty… of your days," Ka said. Luna stared at him along with the others. "It will take… thirty… of your days. Am I… saying it right?"

Luna hoped not, but she worried that he was. They'd been preparing an army for a war, but now it sounded as though they only had a month in which to win it, and if they didn't…

…if they didn't, then their entire planet would be torn apart.

CHAPTER ELEVEN

Kevin sat in the bulbous cabin of the *Dart,* hands gripping onto the arms of the seat as he tried not to show any of the worry that he felt. Around him, the Ilari whom General s'Lara had selected for the mission sat in their own chairs, when they weren't working to suggest course corrections for the ship. Ro and Chloe were there too, held into contoured seats by padding that surrounded them perfectly, adapting as they moved.

"Is everyone ready?" General s'Lara asked.

Kevin nodded. "I am."

They needed to get back. They needed to return to Earth if they were going to have a chance of stopping all of this. One by one, he saw the others nod, and that felt good. He needed to know that the ones taking part in this wanted to be here.

"These are the best we have," General s'Lara said. "Each one is one of our finest fighters, linked to some of our strongest AIs. Once we arrive, the rest of the fleet will be following behind. They will be moving at maximum speed, and if we are lucky…"

"If we're lucky, they won't miss the fight completely," Chloe guessed. She didn't sound as though she thought it was likely.

General s'Lara nodded. "For now, we must treat it as if they will not arrive. Even pushing themselves hard, it will take time to reach Earth. Get ready, everyone. The hangar doors are opening."

Above, Kevin could see the roof of the hangar splitting apart to reveal the sky above. He could see the blueness of it spread out like the oceans that this world seemed to lack on the surface. Below him, he could feel the rumble of the engines as they fired, the shaking of the ship as the energy fields of the ship started to lift it from the launch pad.

General s'Lara seemed to be the one in control of the ship, although, since she was doing it through her AI, it was hard to tell for sure. She sat there, her hands tapping at the air the way Kevin might have at a computer keyboard.

In response to her movements, the *Dart* leapt up to meet the sky. Kevin saw clouds race toward them, then past them, the sky shifting in color as they ripped through the layers of the atmosphere. It was hard for him to keep up with the sheer speed of it all, the sky moving from light blue to midnight, to deepest black in a matter of moments. In the space beyond the world, Kevin could see the remains of the Ilari fleet hanging there, turning with what seemed like a ponderous lack of speed toward their next destination.

"They're all so slow," Chloe said, and Kevin was glad that it wasn't just him seeing it.

"The *Dart*'s engines are already starting to distort things," General s'Lara said. "We are shifting from one reality to the next, so things appear slower out there."

Already, Kevin could feel the speed they were moving at. The Hive's world ship was probably almost as fast, but it didn't feel fast in the same way that the *Dart* did. Maybe the sheer scale of the world ship made it somehow more stable, or maybe it was a quirk of the gravity drives that the Hive used, but it felt so smooth when it was moving that it hardly seemed to be doing it.

The *Dart,* by contrast, thrust forward toward the stars, shaking and juddering with the sheer speed and energy involved as it went. Several of the Ilari had looks of concentration as they conversed with their AIs, obviously trying to get them to compensate for that. Looking back, Kevin could see the Ilari planet receding into the distance, the green of it like an emerald against the black.

It went faster, and faster still, the stars in front blurring with the speed.

"Engaging shift drives," General s'Lara said.

Now the space ahead shifted in color, from black to an entire rainbow of streaking hues. As it flickered past, it seemed to be doing it at impossible speeds now, the ship not just skipping across space but ripping through it as well.

The speed and power of the ship pressed Kevin back into his seat with almost crushing force. He suspected that the ship's shields were doing a lot to protect everyone within from the forces involved, but even so, the acceleration made it hard for him to breathe. He couldn't have done this if he'd still been ill. If the aliens hadn't cured him, he would never have survived this journey.

"It's not done yet," Kevin reminded himself.

The ship was shaking more now, rattling with the forces it was generating, sounding as though it was about to pull itself apart at any moment.

"We're getting turbulence from the dimensional shifts," one of the Ilari said. "We need to slow down, General."

"If we slow ourselves, we won't make Earthfall in time," she replied, before Kevin could say anything. "There's no point in getting there if the planet is already destroyed. We *need* this way to win."

"We could stop," Kevin said. "You shouldn't risk your lives for us."

General s'Lara shook her head in response to that. "We're committed to this. Besides, the way the shift drive works would make that dangerous. If we drop out from the dimensions without planning it, we could end up anywhere."

Kevin wasn't sure he liked the sound of that, especially with the way the ship was starting to creak and squeal in response to every move it made.

"Is this going to hold together?" Chloe asked. She sounded afraid, and Kevin could definitely understand that fear. The *Dart* felt as though it might be about to fall apart at any moment.

"There's no way of knowing," General s'Lara said. "I wish I could be more comforting, but this is an experimental ship, and… *damn!*"

Alarms started to go off within the cockpit, blaring loud enough that they hurt Kevin's ears. Lights flashed, and Kevin had a feeling that none of it was good.

"What's happening?" Kevin asked.

"I'm not sure," General s'Lara said, and in their own way, those were probably the most worrying words that she could have said. "Problems in the lower right quadrant with one of the shield drives. If it fails, the whole ship could be unbalanced."

"How bad is that?" Kevin asked.

"Bad."

General s'Lara signaled to a couple of the other Ilari, who stood and headed for a door at the back of the cockpit. They moved with the kind of urgency that said they had no time to spare or explain or do anything other than try to fix this before it got worse.

All Kevin could do was sit in his chair, pinned in place by the force of the flight, watching down the length of the *Dart* in the hope that everything would be all right. Because he was watching, he saw the moment when a part of the hull collapsed, tearing off and spinning out into the multicolored space beyond. Figures flew from it, and Kevin felt a pang of guilt and regret that people who had come to help him were dying like that. He wanted to save them. He wanted to help them.

"There has to be something we can do," Kevin called out.

General s'Lara seemed to be too busy trying to wrestle with the unseen controls of the ship to answer for a moment. Kevin felt the ship lurching beneath him, starting to spin so that the sights beyond the ship rotated almost too fast to follow.

"Someone take the controls!" she yelled. "Kevin, Chloe, Ro, my people need to hold the ship so it doesn't get lost between dimensions. We need to make sure it doesn't fall apart. Come with me. Hurry."

She set off toward the rear of the ship and Kevin rose to follow her. It took more effort than he could have believed just to step out of the chair, the pressure of the ship's movement threatening to squash him down in place.

"Can we do anything to help the people who fell from the ship?" Kevin asked.

General s'Lara shook her head. "We'll be lucky if we can even save ourselves. With just the fields we have—"

"Would a gravity field help?" Ro asked.

"It might," General s'Lara said. "But to produce one… *could* we produce one?"

"My field was reshaping flesh," Ro said, "but I believe I know enough to see how your shields could be adapted. We will have to act fast though."

The alien led the way through the ship now, and Kevin followed as quickly as he could, given the effort required. Chloe put a hand on his arm. It was the hand with the alien device wrapped around it, and her grip was stronger than Kevin had expected. Together, they pushed their way forward, moving deeper into the ship's interior, to a space where a door stood waiting.

"My AI says that the space beyond this is vacuum," General s'Lara said. "If there were more time, we would construct robots for the repairs, but there isn't. We've managed to get a partial shield in place to seal the breach, and your suits will shield you against a vacuum for a time, but we will still have to work fast."

Kevin nodded, then looked across to Ro. "What do we need to do?"

"I'll know once we're in there," the alien said. "Although you and Chloe should stay. It might be dangerous in there."

"It's dangerous *anywhere* in the ship if we don't solve this," Chloe pointed out.

Kevin nodded. "Chloe's right. We're helping."

General s'Lara moved to the door and it slid open. Kevin felt his suit adjust, a flickering shield popping into existence around his head. He could feel forces pulling at him, trying to drag him through, and he had to grab for the doorway to hold himself in place. On the far side of the room, a section of the hull stood open to the space beyond, ragged as a wound.

"Yes, I think that we can do this," Ro said. "I will need to describe things to your... machine, but we can work with this. Those connectors will need to be reattached when I say, not before."

"We'll do it," Kevin said, following the line of Ro's pointing finger. Two large, plug-like things sat disconnected from sockets, while a tangle of wires sat near them.

"General, I'll tell you what to do while I work," the alien said.

"You get that one, and I'll get the one on the far side," Chloe said to Kevin.

He nodded, and started to make his way across the room. It was hard; so hard that each step seemed to take an eternity, the combined force of the ship's speed and the pulling vacuum beyond it. Each step was a fight, the soles of his boots clamping to the floor, but the moments in between requiring complete concentration just to push forward.

Kevin could see Chloe dragging herself forward using a combination of the curious strength that the Hive's reshaping had given her and the grip given to her by her altered arm. Ro was working among the tangled wires, apparently braced against a large piece of machinery. General s'Lara seemed almost to be communing with some of the machinery, whispering to it while parts of it started to reconfigure themselves.

"Quickly, Kevin," Ro said. "We must do this at the right moment."

Kevin pressed forward, taking another step, and another, forcing himself to hurry. He felt the moment when his foot slipped, pressing forward a little too far and too fast. He felt the moment when the vacuum pulled at him, dragging him from the deck toward the hole in the ship's outer skin.

He saw the space outside rushing up to meet him, and then he felt fingers closing around his. Strong fingers, powerful fingers, and not quite human in the roughness of their grip. Chloe's altered arm clamped around his, holding Kevin in place while his legs dangled from the hole in the ship, threatening to drag him into the beyond.

Kevin clung to her and pulled himself back down onto the deck, feeling his boots connect to the surface and stick there.

"Hurry, both of you," Ro called out.

Kevin remembered what he was supposed to be doing. They needed to make the connections at the right time, or this wouldn't work.

"Quick," he called to Chloe, and started for his chosen cable again. He wished there was enough time to be careful, but he had to hurry even more now. He pushed forward against the drag of the vacuum, reaching for the connector with both hands. He grabbed it and lifted, feeling its weight.

"Now!" Ro called.

Kevin jammed the connector into place and heard the hum as the machinery started. Kevin saw energy fields flicker around the ship and felt the path of the vessel smooth out, so that it was no longer an effort to move across the floor.

"It's working," General s'Lara said. "We can get the ship back where it should be. Come on. We might not make it to Earth before the Hive, but we can get there before it is destroyed."

She rushed through to the control room, and Kevin followed with the others. The Ilari seemed more relaxed now, as if they were able to work on controlling the *Dart* more easily. They moved forward through spaces that seemed to have nothing to do with the universe Kevin knew. The ship rushed forward, driven by a combination of Ilari and Hive technology.

"We're getting close," General s'Lara said. "We'll drop out of this shifting space soon, and then we'll have to find a way past any Hive ships that are still there. Hold on. With the change to the drives, the rate of braking might be affected. You're going to want to be in your seats."

Kevin got back into his, feeling the padding wrapping around him to hold him in place as the ship started to slow down.

"It's taking longer than anticipated," General s'Lara said. Kevin could hear the worried note there, and that seemed like a bad thing, given how calmly she'd taken control with the ship falling apart.

The sky outside the ship drifted down into shades of black from the unnatural colors it had turned. Kevin saw shapes flickering by, and he recognized asteroids, the round shapes of planets, the fiery mass of the sun in the distance.

The Earth was there, getting closer by the second, the Hive's world ship hanging over it in silent threat.

"Pull up," Kevin whispered, willing the ship to slow faster. "Pull *up*."

"The ship is too damaged," General s'Lara said. "I can't control the speed of our descent enough. I think… I think that we're going to hit your planet."

CHAPTER TWELVE

Too fast—the ship was moving too fast. Kevin could see the world rising up to meet the *Dart*, its pole like the bull's-eye of a dartboard, growing larger by the second. He could feel panic rising, and around him, some of the Ilari were screaming.

They were going to crash.

"We need to pull up!" General s'Lara shouted, and Kevin knew that she had to be shouting at her AI.

He could feel the ship beneath him fighting to do what the general wanted. He could feel it fighting to level out, while around the cockpit of the ship, Kevin could see the red-orange glow of it heating up as it hit the atmosphere.

"We're coming in too steeply," General s'Lara said.

"What does that mean?" Chloe asked, from her chair.

Ro answered. "If we don't level out, even the shields won't keep us from burning up like a meteorite."

The pressure was back as they plunged toward the world, smashing Kevin back against his seat while the ship tried to level out, slow down... *anything*. He saw the glow outside go from orange to blue, to white, the shields rippling with it.

Slowly, though, so slowly that it seemed to take an eternity, the glow receded. But they didn't stop falling. The ground was still coming up toward them far too fast, and the ship didn't seem to be doing anything to stop it.

"Strap yourselves in!" General s'Lara shouted. "The ship is using full reverse thrust, but... we're going to hit."

They plunged toward the ground, and below them, Kevin briefly saw snow-covered trees, and mountaintops that came far too close to the underside of the *Dart*. He even thought he felt something scrape along the bottom of the already damaged ship, but that might have been his imagination.

Ahead, there was water, and an endless expanse of whiteness. It was only as the landscape passed beneath that Kevin got a true idea of the speed at which they were traveling, slowing by the second, but still moving far too fast to land safely.

They didn't.

Kevin felt the underside of the ship scrape along a ridge of ice and snow, then the whole thing flipped, tumbling down and rolling, the world flashing past in a circling whirl that Kevin couldn't keep up with. It was snow, and then sky, and then snow again, until beneath them, Kevin heard something crack.

The ship plunged down through a sheet of ice, and now water surrounded it, pressing in on all sides as it plunged into lightless depths. It bumped against something and held, so tentatively that for a moment or two, Kevin didn't even dare to breathe. Only when he was sure that it was still did he gasp in air, trying not to let fear at what was happening overwhelm him.

"We're at the bottom of the ocean," Chloe said.

General s'Lara shook her head. "Not the bottom. Sensors say that we have hit a rock shelf attached to one of this world landmasses, and that the ship is currently stable, although it will take the rest of the fleet to salvage any of it."

"And in the meantime, we're stuck underwater?" Kevin asked. He shook his head; he knew that wouldn't work. They wouldn't have enough food, or air, to simply wait. Around them, he could see bubbles of air rising, heading toward light so far above that it might have been on a different world.

Besides, they needed to get back home, back to where all of this would be fought out. Back to Luna.

"How many people are injured?" Ro asked. It was a question that Kevin knew he should have asked, and he was quite surprised that the former member of the Hive had managed to beat him to it.

"Numerous minor injuries," General s'Lara said. "Six more serious, two fatalities. With a reduced crew aboard, the ship should have enough resources for those who remain until we can rescue them."

She seemed to take it for granted that they would find a way out of there, and that they would manage to find a way to win this. Kevin would have hated to be one of those left behind, not knowing if anyone would ever come back for them, if the ship would be recoverable, or if they would find themselves left to sit on the bottom until they either starved or suffocated.

Maybe it was still easier than what they were going to have to do.

"How do we get out of here?" Kevin asked. "What do we do, when we… where *are* we?"

General s'Lara pointed to a screen, which now showed a map of the Earth. "According to the sensors, we are here." She pointed to a spot in the far north, up in the white glaze of the Arctic. It was a spot that was blue on the map, just on the edge of frozen land. "We need to move south, to a place called Los Angeles. There are reports of an attempt to fight the Hive there, and of a human girl leading an army that knows how to take them on."

"Luna," Kevin and Chloe said at the same time, looking across at one another. There could be any number of other girls it could be, but somehow, Kevin knew that it wasn't one of them. It was too much of a coincidence if it was some other girl. Only Luna would be able to unite an army behind her against the aliens.

Of course, Kevin thought with a sudden deflation of his hopes, the last time he'd seen Luna, she'd been controlled by the Hive.

"Whoever it is," Ro said, "connecting with them represents our best opportunity. Is it far?"

"Thousands of miles," Kevin said.

"We will gain transport," General s'Lara said. "We will make it there in time."

"We still have to make it off the ship," Chloe pointed out.

"That part, at least, is easy enough. Your suits will protect you from the vacuum of space. A little water is not a problem."

Kevin wished he had her confidence. She made the frozen waste of the Arctic sound like it was nothing, rather than the kind of place that could kill someone in a matter of moments if they made a mistake there.

"We will get to the surface," the general declared, "assess our surroundings, and take up what equipment we can for the fight ahead. Kevin, Chloe, Ro, come with me. I want to see what this world of yours is like."

She led the way back through the ship, pausing so that the three of them could collect their weapons as they had before, and then demonstrating how the field on her suit formed a kind of air tight bubble around her. She made it all sound so normal and so safe, but even so, Kevin was sure that there were about a thousand things that could go wrong with this. They were about to step out into freezing water, into a world that had nothing to do with the beautiful greenery of the Ilari's home.

"We will use airlock B," General s'Lara said. "It is pointing toward the surface, so it should just be a question of swimming straight up."

Should. It was such a small word, but it carried a lot with it. Kevin could hear in the general's voice that she wasn't sure, not entirely. What other option did they have though? They couldn't stay there. They *had* to get up to the surface.

They made it to airlock B, stepping inside together. The strangest part about it was that when the outer door pulled back, there was still just a shimmering wall of water beyond, held back by the Ilari's shield technology. Kevin could see the pale light at the surface now.

"Once you get outside, *swim*," General s'Lara said. "We need to get to the surface."

"And if the ice has sealed over the surface?" Ro asked.

General s'Lara hefted her weapon. "Then we blast our way through. Ready?"

She didn't wait for an answer before stepping through. Ro stepped out to follow her, swimming awkwardly.

"Ready?" Kevin asked Chloe.

She took his hand for a moment. "Ready."

Kevin stepped out of the airlock with Chloe, and he saw the fields around his suit flare as they worked to push out the water. He could see dark shapes further off in the water, and he couldn't remember if there were sharks in waters this cold. Then he remembered that even if there weren't, there might still be orca, or leopard seals, or worse.

He kicked up through the water, feeling some of the cold of it, but not all. Kevin guessed that was down to his suit as well, and he didn't want to think about what it might be like if he weren't wearing it. There was even air trapped inside the shield, so that Kevin could breathe as he made his way upward, but he wasn't sure just how long that air would last, or how long he would be able to hold his breath once it ran out.

He made his way up toward the surface, seeing what appeared to be an endless wall of white above him. It was further than it looked, and now he could feel his arms and legs growing tired. So soon after the landing, it seemed like too much to demand of his body, but the alternative was falling back into the dark water and hoping that he could make it to the ship before his air ran out.

Kevin was still thinking about that when a dark shape approached through the water, rushing at him.

The killer whale came closer with almost unbelievable speed, its tail flicking as it propelled itself through the water. Kevin saw its mouth open wide, rows of teeth visible amid the black and white.

A blast of energy from Chloe's pistol fired near it, sending it banking off. Even so, Kevin felt the wash of its strength as it passed close by. Kevin kicked up hard, trying to get to the surface before the creature could attack again. How long would it take the whale to turn? How long before…

It flashed through the water again, and this time, Kevin was the one to fire at it, with the short rifle, again missing by the narrowest of margins as it flitted away.

"Is it gone?" Chloe asked.

Kevin shook his head. "I doubt it. We need to get up there."

They headed for the ice above, a solid sheet now that was translucent in the places where it was thinner and a deep blue-white where it was thick. General s'Lara must have broken through there somewhere, but Kevin couldn't find the spot. Instead, he came up against the ice, where there was the smallest of gaps between the ice and the waves, so Kevin was able to poke his head up to get a brief breath of fresh air.

He thought he could see something circling below in the darkness. He lifted his rifle, aiming not at the whale, but at the ice above. He fired, holding down the trigger and feeling more than hearing the boom of the ice as it hit. Ice flew in every direction, some of it flying back through the water like shrapnel.

Sunlight glistened above, a ragged hole in the ice giving Kevin a way out. He clambered onto the ice, digging in with his gun so that he could pull himself out despite the slipperiness. He rolled onto his back, staring up at a gray sky that was howling with wind.

"Kevin! Kevin, help!" Chloe called. Kevin looked over to see that she was struggling at the edge of the ice hole, not able to pull herself out. He couldn't see the whale in the water, heading up toward her, but he knew that it would be.

"I'm coming," he yelled, running over. His feet started to slip, and for a moment, Kevin thought he would end up falling into the water with her. Instead, he threw himself down flat, reaching out for Chloe from what seemed like the first of the solid ice.

His hand clamped around her wrist, and he pulled, dragging her forward inch by inch. He could see Chloe struggling, trying to get her legs onto dry land. Kevin managed to yank her forward, and they both tumbled back onto the ice. An instant later, the head of the killer whale came thundering up out of the hole. It blew water from its blowhole and dipped back beneath the ice with a clicking squeal.

General s'Lara and Ro were further off on the ice, sitting up on it and looking around as if they couldn't quite believe what they were seeing. Kevin realized that this was their first view from the surface of his world. It probably wasn't what they'd been expecting.

"Is all your world like this?" General s'Lara asked.

Kevin shook his head. "This is the Arctic. The rest of the world… there's so much here."

"I look forward to seeing it."

"We need to live that long first," Ro said, with a glance toward the ominous clouds above. Kevin could see what he meant—the clouds seemed to be closing in fast, the winds rising until they howled along the ice.

Slowly, one by one, Ilari started to surface from beneath it. Most struggled up to the surface. Some brought equipment with them, and all brought weapons. Some were bleeding. One… one had most of a leg missing, and tumbled back into the water, a dark form rising behind him.

Kevin raised his weapon and fired down into the water, not knowing if he hit the whale or not.

"There's no time," General s'Lara said. "We need to get to true land before this storm hits."

Kevin looked around, trying to make sense of the place they were in. They appeared to be in the middle of an ice floe, but Kevin could see what seemed like a field of thicker ice, chunks of it sticking out like teeth from the ground.

"There," he said, and General s'Lara nodded.

They ran for the ice field, making their way through the snow and ice as fast as it would let them. It wasn't quickly though, and they had to struggle for grip with every step, fighting to make progress, and hopping between slender gaps in the ice sheets. Kevin's breath was so cold now that it hurt, in spite of the warmth of his suit. They needed to get to shelter.

The first snow of the storm hit in a vertical wall of white. Kevin, Chloe, and the others ran for the limited cover of the icefield.

"Dig down into the snow," General s'Lara called out. "My AI suggests that it is our best chance for warmth. Use your weapons to cut space."

Kevin nodded, and he turned his gun on the space beneath one of the large blocks of ice. It burned away the snow and ice, turning the top layers to steam. The hole that it cut was too small to call a real shelter, too small to call more than the hole it was. Even so, the ice and snow around it provided shelter from the wind, and meant that the heat from him and his suit could start to fill it.

As the worst of the snow started to fall, Kevin hunkered down in it and hoped that the heat would be enough.

CHAPTER THIRTEEN

Kevin woke to whiteness that seemed to fill everything, and a cold that pierced through him like a hundred knives. He blinked, and ice crystals fell from his eyes. A part of him wanted to hunker down further, seeking warmth in the snow. A part of him wanted to just close his eyes again, even though the rest knew of him that he couldn't; that doing it would be death, even with the protection of the suit he wore.

He forced himself to stretch out an arm, digging his way through the snow ahead of him. It was so thick that it felt like a wall, and Kevin had to force his arms to keep moving, digging through the snowfall until they finally burst through into the light.

Kevin sucked in cold air, dragging himself out into the ice field. He looked around, seeing Chloe's transformed arm flailing in the air. He helped her to dig her way free, while a little way further on, Ro pulled his way from his shelter.

"I think I prefer the days when I could feel nothing," the alien muttered.

"No you don't," Kevin said, because he knew what it had been like as one of the Hive. Even the fear, and the cold, and the rest of it were better than the empty *nothing* of being a part of the Hive's structure.

"No," Ro agreed, "I don't."

General s'Lara came out of the snow a little further off. Around Kevin, Ilari started to emerge from their sheltered spots, rising up out of them and shaking off the snow. Not all of them did, though. Kevin could see the spots where Ilari lay on the ice, frozen in death, or where the snow holes had stayed frozen over.

"It hurts every time," the general said.

Kevin nodded. He felt hurt too, and knew it must only be a tiny fraction of the grief that the general was feeling. He felt responsible for bringing the Ilari, and could only guess at how responsible General s'Lara would feel when she was the one who had given the actual commands.

Kevin was surprised to feel himself growing warmer.

"Your suit will work with the energy from your star," General s'Lara said. "In extreme conditions though, it can be... worn down."

Kevin could hear the hurt there.

86

"I'm sorry," he said.

General s'Lara shook her head. "Don't be sorry; just promise me that their sacrifice won't be in vain. Make sure that we *win* this."

Kevin wished that he could promise it, but, looking up at the Hive's world ship, it was hard. There was too much chance that they might lose this. There were still too many things that might go wrong.

"We know what the Hive came here for," he said. "We have your weaponry, and the material that they've been looking for. We can *do* this."

"Only if we can get to LA," Chloe pointed out. "It's a long way."

"We can arrange transport," General s'Lara said, and turned to the others. "Bring out the skidders."

The Ilari who had brought up equipment started to drag out curved plates of silvery metal. They looked a little like the golden discs that the Hive used to move about in the world ship, but since the Ilari didn't have the gravity technology the Hive had, they relied on powerful-looking engines that they attached to them.

The aliens worked quickly and efficiently, but Kevin could see that some of them had grim expressions, obviously hurt by how many of their number had already died on this mission. It made them seem better than the Hive, because when they chose to risk their lives, it came down to more than logic. They knew how much their lives meant, and they still chose to be a part of this.

"Here," General s'Lara said, pointing to one of the large plates. It looked like the kind of paper airplane someone might have made if they had worked with metal, or maybe like a silvery hovercraft without the skirt. "This one will respond to touch, so you and Chloe should take it."

"We're getting one for ourselves?" Kevin said.

"There is still an AI aboard," the general explained. "Ro, you are with me."

Kevin climbed onto the skidder, and Chloe clambered on behind him. Kevin could see a couple of patches of the metal that looked like handprints, and as he reached out to touch them, he felt the engines roar into life. The vehicle lifted above the ice, not quite to the level that a spaceship might have, but still high enough that he hoped he didn't fall.

Gingerly, he tried adjusting the pressure of his hands, and the craft lurched forward, then slid to the side. He tried more smoothly, and now Kevin felt as though he understood the controls he held.

They were so simple and intuitive that within seconds, Kevin felt as if the vehicle was almost a part of him.

Around him, the Ilari started to form up on their own craft, bringing them up to the same height as Kevin. General s'Lara's vehicle was next to him at the head of their formation, obviously waiting for something. It took Kevin a moment to realize what.

"I'm ready," he said. "Let's go."

They shot south, so fast that for a moment or two, Kevin thought he might be torn from the craft as it flew. He should have known better than that, though, when it came to the Ilari. Energy flared around the craft, deflecting small particles as they struck the shields that formed a bubble around it, making sure that neither Kevin nor Chloe fell off as it rocketed a little way above the surface of the landscape.

He shot between ice boulders and occasional giant mounds of snow. A stretch of open water lay ahead, and Kevin didn't slow down. Instead, his vehicle skimmed above the waves, moving faster than any car or bike could have on a road. Trees lay ahead, and now the vehicles picked their way between them, making their way through the few openings that lay there. The AI in the craft must have been assisting Kevin, because it felt completely natural to slalom through the trees at impossible speeds.

They kept going south, and now Kevin could see the beginnings of settlements here and there, all looking abandoned, because there would have been nowhere to hide from the vapor when it came.

They kept going, because there was nothing to do there, and this was about saving the whole world.

The landscape flashed past now, the sun moving in the sky as the hours passed. The worst part for Kevin was not knowing what was happening down in LA. As fast as they were moving, were they going fast enough? Would they be able to get there before things went too far to save anything? Was Luna safe?

All Kevin could do was keep pushing forward, and hope.

***

"How far now?" Kevin called over to General s'Lara as they kept heading south. The snow seemed to be giving way to warmer land, with hints of green among it, and the first signs of real roads.

"Still a long way," General s'Lara said. "Even at this speed, the journey will take many hours. If we had been able to approach smoothly from orbit, then I would have… damn it."

Kevin looked in the direction that she was looking, and it took him a moment or two to realize just what the general was looking at. A metal thing hung in the air there, circular and more than the size of a person. It had spikes sticking out that looked like probes, and it seemed to be keeping pace with them.

"I recognize that," Ro said, from the back of General s'Lara's skidder. "The Hive uses probes like that in spaces where it has no creatures to see."

"And it has seen us," General s'Lara said. "Our AIs might be able to stall the signal for a minute or two, but—"

"Do it," Kevin called out, and then sent his skidder after the probe. He glanced back at Chloe, who had her pistol ready without being asked. "If I get us close enough, can you shoot it?"

"Just catch it," Chloe replied.

They skimmed across the landscape, moving even faster now than they had, at a speed that Kevin was sure the craft wouldn't be able to maintain for long. That didn't matter, though. If the Hive learned that they were there before they got into place to help, then they would send every resource they had against them. The enemy would pick them off before they even got to the battle they were planning on having.

They had to stop it.

Kevin guided the skidder out toward the probe, and now it seemed to be running ahead of them, well designed enough at least to know that it needed to escape to deliver its report. It was moving erratically, changing direction seemingly at random, trying to catch them moving the wrong way so that it could get clear and send its message.

Kevin and Chloe shot through a stand of trees, then out over an outcrop of rock. The probe shot up and then across a lake, but they followed, not letting it out of their sight. Chloe fired at the probe, shooting over Kevin's shoulder, but they were too far away and her shots went wide. They needed to be close if this was going to work.

"It's pulling away," Chloe said.

Kevin shook his head. They weren't going to let it escape.

He watched the probe as he drove the skidder, trying to keep up with it, but also trying to do more than that. If it was a machine, then it couldn't be truly random, could it? It could only do the things that it had been programmed to do. There had to be a pattern to it.

Suddenly, Kevin knew what it was going to do next.

"What are you doing?" Chloe called out as Kevin jerked the skidder to the right. "We're going to lose it!"

"Trust me!" Kevin yelled back, continuing on the course he'd picked. He shot through another stand of trees, keeping deliberately low, deliberately out of sight. Kevin raced through, hoping that he had judged this right. If he hadn't, then the whole of the Hive would come down on them, and there was no hope that any of them would survive.

Ahead, all he saw was emptiness.

"No," Kevin said. "Come *on*."

Had he misjudged it? Had he just gone off in a random direction, and lost the probe that they needed to catch? A sinking feeling started to spread in the pit of his stomach.

Then he saw the dot approaching along the line of the trees, quickly resolving itself into the shape of the alien device. He waited until he couldn't wait any longer, and then sent the skidder shooting forward once again.

Instantly, they were close to the probe. Kevin saw the flickers of energy as Chloe shot at it again, and this time, some of the shots hit home. The probe slowed slightly, but there was no sign of damage on it.

"It's not working," Chloe said. "We need to try something else."

"Maybe we're still too far," Kevin suggested.

"Maybe…" Chloe said. She sounded as though she was planning something. "Just how close can you get?"

Kevin didn't know, but he was determined to find out. He pushed the skidder as hard as he could, sending it closer moment by moment while Chloe continued to fire to slow the probe down. He could predict its moves now, and that meant that he could turn just that little bit sharper, get there just before the probe did.

It didn't take long before they were almost on top of it.

"Are we close enough yet?" Kevin asked, not knowing how close they needed to be for whatever Chloe was thinking of.

"I think so," Chloe replied. "Just… just make sure that you catch me!"

Before Kevin could turn and ask her what she meant, she leapt from the skidder, crossing the distance between the two vehicles in a jump that seemed far more than human. It appeared that she was making full use of whatever the Hive had done to her. She arced through the air, then landed on the probe, clinging to its spines as though it were some bizarre, circular steed.

She seemed to have abandoned her pistol, holding her shock baton instead and tearing at the spines of the probe until she had pulled the metal apart enough to expose the device's inner workings. She lifted her baton high, and in that moment, Kevin realized what she meant about him catching her.

She plunged the baton down, and power crackled down into the probe. The device hung in the air, and Chloe seemed rigid too, the surface conducting just enough of the power of the shock baton to stun. She toppled back from it just as the probe started to tumble from the air.

Kevin ignored the device, lancing the skidder down, not caring that it was taking him toward hard rocks. All that mattered was getting in between Chloe and the ground. He pushed the silvery surface down until he thought it might rip it from him, then held out a searching hand…

His hand caught hold of Chloe, dragging her back onto the skidder.

By then, it was too late to stop completely, but the AI was already working to pull the skidder up. It meant that, even as the probe crashed to the ground in a ball of flames, the skidder touched down and slid along the ground like a sled. Kevin put his hands back to the controls and pulled at them, succeeding in raising it up into the sky.

He looked round. Behind him, Chloe was groaning, her eyelids fluttering open.

"Did it work?" she asked. "Did I stop it?"

"You did," Kevin assured her. "That was awesome!" He brought the skidder around so that Chloe could see the wreckage of the probe. He flew deliberately low so he could snatch up her stun baton, passing it to her.

"That's good. I think… I think I'll sleep for a bit now."

"You do that," Kevin said. He thought she'd earned it. Ahead, he could see General s'Lara and the others, moving round to meet them.

"You've saved us," the general said. "Both of you. We can continue to head for LA in stealth. Perhaps we will even have the advantage of surprise for this battle."

Talk of the battle to come made Kevin pause. It was a reminder that it had just taken them everything they had to stop one probe, and there would be far more aliens to come. They needed to get to LA, and they were running out of time.

CHAPTER FOURTEEN

Luna hid among the buildings of LA, waiting for the alien squad to get close, trying to be still among the ruins of the city. Any movement now might give them away, and they couldn't afford that. Beside her, Bobby made a low, growling sound. Luna put a hand on the dog's head.

"Quiet, Bobby. Not yet."

This was a large force, with phalanxes of the controlled, but also plenty of real aliens, in so many forms that it seemed impossible to keep track of them all. There were spiderlike things and great hairy beasts, black-armored soldiers and slender creatures that moved fast, scuttling along buildings while holding guns.

"Looks as though they've started to take us seriously," Leon whispered, moving up beside Luna.

"It's probably because we're taking mines back from them," Luna replied.

"Or because the people they're controlling are waking up, thanks to you," Leon suggested.

Luna shook her head. "Thanks to all of us."

How did you conduct a war against an alien threat that was so powerful? The answer, it turned out, was that you took away what the aliens wanted. Luna and her army had set about trying to take away the mineral wherever they could find it, and the message about the cure seemed to be spreading too. Now when the Survivors scavenged for resources they were as likely to meet ordinary, cured people as the controlled.

There was still a long way to go, though. The Hive were starting to fight back. Luna's people making their bases in the quarries where the minerals could be found helped, because it meant that the aliens couldn't just target them with their weapons for fear of setting off exactly the kind of reaction that converted their people. Even so, a group like this proved how much the Hive wanted to keep control of the Earth until they had stripped it of its resources.

"Wait for it," Luna said, trying to judge the perfect moment to strike out at the aliens in front of them. "Wait for it… *now!*"

She stood up, throwing out a lump of the mineral, and a black-armored figure shot at it from cover. The first shot missed, but the second slammed into the mineral, detonating it and flattening a huge swath of the advancing enemy force.

Instantly, everything turned to chaos, enemies firing blindly back at them, while Luna's forces shot with dart guns and slingshots, anything that could carry the cure. They fired into the middle of the controlled, even though it would probably have been better to target the aliens first. The truth was that all her forces had an easier time shooting at aliens with their real weapons than at anything human, and Luna... well, she wished that no one had to die because of the Hive's cruelty, but wars weren't fought like that.

"We've finished the first barrage," Leon said.

Sometimes this was the point where they pulled back, but Luna could see that there were still too many aliens standing for that. Some were standing blinking, trying to work out what was going on, but too many others were charging, or firing back at her people, or just trying to corral the former controlled. If their forces stopped now, then all the people who had just been cured would simply be ripped apart instead.

"Okay," Luna shouted. "Fire!"

Now the rest of her forces opened up with their weaponry, and it was an increasingly powerful collection thanks to the aliens they'd managed to cure. Some held energy weapons, others gravity-powered devices that could accelerate stones to impossible speeds. The Survivors had a growing collection of guns of all kinds, and those rattled and barked, firing down at any enemy who still seemed to be attacking them.

Plenty fell in those first barrages, and plenty more started to fall as the cure took effect, turning more and more of the Hive's forces against the rest. Luna's people continued to fire down with darts and with globes packed with the cure, while she hefted another precious lump of the mineral, ready to throw.

"Wait until there's a threat that needs it," Leon suggested.

A part of Luna wanted to throw the rock anyway, but she held back for now. She was quickly grateful that she had, as a low, broad, tank-like vehicle hovered into view, weapons bristling from it. An energy cannon fired, and a group of Luna's people found themselves vaporized instantly. Another shot, and a section of building collapsed, far too close.

"I need to get near it," Luna yelled. "Someone be ready to fire!"

She ran for the hover tank, keeping in cover as much as she could. The thing seemed to track her, as if sensing that Luna was the danger there. A blast struck a building near her, sending fragments of stone flying and forcing her to duck. Bobby barked and pushed at her, reminding her to keep moving.

Luna ducked through a doorway ahead of another blast. She threw herself across a passageway while energy ripped through it. A spiked, insectoid thing rose up in front of her and for a moment, Luna thought that she might have to fight it, but then a shot came from behind her, punching through the thing's carapace.

She was getting close to the hover tank now. Around her, Luna could see the battle continuing, with flickers of energy fire shooting back and forth from the ground to the surrounding buildings. She kept low, and Bobby slunk along at her side, almost on his belly.

One of the controlled leapt out at Luna, and Bobby sprang at him, snapping and snarling, giving Luna enough time to drag a syringe from her belt and plunge it home in the man. He collapsed, his eyes rolling back in his head, and Luna knew that it wouldn't be long before he woke again as the man he had once been.

For now, though, she needed to focus on the tank.

Another cascade of energy told her its location, and now Luna guessed that she was close enough. She popped out from behind the walls that had given her cover, holding the lump of mineral ready to throw. She waited for the barrel of its main weapon to turn to her, and then she flung the rock straight down it, sprinting for cover.

The explosion rippled out, its transforming wave washing over the aliens still controlled by the Hive. Luna threw herself flat, feeling the shockwave pass over, then stood, trying to get a sense of the rest of the battle.

By this point, there *was* no more battle. They'd won their skirmish, and there wasn't a figure there that wasn't either standing around wondering what was happening, or running for sanctuary elsewhere. Either way, they weren't controlled by the Hive anymore. Luna could see the men and women there congratulating one another on the victory, some cheering, some clapping one another on the back or punching the air. Luna hated to be the one to kill the mood, but she knew that she had to.

"We need to get back to the quarry," she called out. "We'll be safe there. Everyone gather up your weapons, and help anyone who is injured. Look after the people next to you."

She saw some of those who had only just been cured still stumbling a little, but being supported by the ones who had helped to bring about the ambush. They moved along en masse, and it occurred to Luna that in a lot of ways, they were doing to the Hive what it did to the worlds it conquered. They were taking new soldiers with every fight, so that their army grew even as the Hive's shrank.

"Come on," Luna called, leading the way back toward the quarry. Their small army moved together, heading back in the direction of safety, however tenuous it might be. They picked their way through the rubble of LA, and Luna wanted to believe that, while they were doing it, a hundred other armies around the world would be doing the same thing. They would be fighting the aliens everywhere by now, taking back their cities stride by stride, converting the people the aliens had taken.

It was a long march, and an exhausting one, if only because of the effort needed to keep so many people moving in the same direction, and focused on the same things. Luna knew the sheer scale of her army meant that she would soon have to think about other things, like food production and keeping order, but for now, she was just grateful that she *had* so many people with her, and that they *could* take on the aliens.

Then the quarry came into sight, and Luna saw the army of aliens surrounding it.

"No," she said. "They wouldn't be stupid enough to attack… the mineral…"

"Look," Leon said, pointing to the sky. Ships hung there in the hundreds, some simply waiting, some striking down with blasts of energy as people tried to leave. "It's not an attack; it's a blockade."

Luna understood then. They were going to pen up her people, effectively holding them hostage, or perhaps just holding them in place so that they could be destroyed from above. Worse, looking up, Luna could see the glow coming from the Hive's world ship. They'd thought that they had thirty days, but how much time had passed now, and how could they be sure that what they thought they knew was true? What if the world ship was already ready to destroy the Earth? What if it would be in just a little while?

Hemmed in, Luna and her people wouldn't be able to do anything to stop it.

"We need to break through that blockade," Luna said. "We need to get our people out of there with as much of the mineral as we can, and then…"

That was the problem. They still hadn't worked out the "and then" part of this. They knew how to convert people. They knew how to use the mineral as a weapon, but they still didn't know how to deal with the Hive ship hanging above them.

That was a problem for another day though. Right then, the only thing to do was to strike out, escape, split up, and get the mineral to as many safe places as possible until they could find a way to use it as a weapon. Perhaps they could put it on a rocket, or find some other way to do this…

For now, there was only one thing to do.

"Attack!" Luna called out, and her army trusted her enough to do it. It didn't matter that some of them were tired, or that they had only just fought another battle. It didn't matter that there were more true aliens there than Luna had seen in one place, or that this would be far more dangerous. They still moved forward.

They fired as they went, shooting with energy beams and darts and slingshots that fired the glass globes with the cure. Luna pulled out the last of her chunks of mineral, trying to judge the best place to throw it, and deciding that the only option that worked was to fling it among a cluster of the tank-like vehicles. She weighed the chunk in her hand and flung it, aiming as close to the center of the group, trusting that one of the soldiers there would be able to target it with an alien weapon.

Shots rang out toward it, and one of them connected, sending a blast rippling out across the aliens' ranks. One of the tanks turned toward the others, blasting out at it with a burst of energy that split it open. Another fired up toward the ships above, winging one of them with a lance of power that made it plummet toward the ground.

Others started to fire back, strafing the ground, firing down toward the ranks of Luna's army.

"Forward!" Luna called out. "We need to get closer to them!"

It was the only place where they might be safe. Out in the open, they would be sitting ducks for the ships. They charged forward, firing with rifles and energy weapons, trying to close in on the Hive's forces. She just had to hope that the ships wouldn't dare to fire down into their own forces.

There was just one problem with that, Luna realized as the ships came around for another run: this was the Hive, and the Hive had no problem with slaughtering its own troops if doing so brought it a step closer to victory.

Energy bursts ripped up the earth along the route toward the fighting armies, then tore into them, apparently without distinguishing between them. More fire came up from the converted tanks, striking more of the ships, but not enough to make a difference, and not enough to change the course of the battle.

Luna saw a large, armor-plated thing charging toward her, and she shot it with a dart gun. It fell back, but there was another one there, and another. People clustered around Luna, forming a hard core of fighters with energy weapons. She waved her hands at them.

"No! Spread out! You're just making yourselves a—"

More energy fire tore down toward them and Luna ran with Bobby, throwing herself to one side as it burst on the spot where she had been standing, sending an explosion bursting up into the air. Plenty of the people with her weren't so lucky. Luna saw Leon lying unmoving on the ground, and couldn't begin to get close enough to help him as a creature rose up above him. Its claws swept down, and Luna had to bite back the urge to shout out as they plunged home.

She saw one of the tanks that they'd converted blown to pieces, and a corridor of aliens cut down. The Hive's superiority in air power was giving it too much of an advantage, so that, whatever happened on the ground, it wouldn't be enough. They would still be picked off.

Worse, Luna looked up from the ground toward the Hive's world ship, and she saw the shadow of city ships in the way. They were gathering like giant rays over the city, three of them together, as if to make certain of this battle.

Luna didn't know what they could do against that. They could kill the aliens fighting them at ground level, and they were, in energy blasts, and explosions, with human guns and alien ones and close combat weapons. They could cure and convert everyone from the controlled to the aliens who came to fought them. Those then fired up with their energy weapons, managing to bring down some, a few, of the smaller ships.

It wasn't enough though. It would never be enough. Even as Luna watched, she could see more of the smaller ships pouring down, presumably bringing more and more of the aliens with them. They poured down in a rain of alien technology and twisted flesh, and somehow, Luna knew that this would be happening all over the rest of the world as well.

Worse, though, above it all, Luna knew that the world ship would be building up its energies. This was a battle that mattered to them, but even if they won now, they might still be destroyed. The whole Earth might. If the aliens had had enough of their pillaging, then there was nothing left but the tearing apart of the planet, and the theft of whatever was left.

Luna stared up in despair, because she was supposed to be the ones with the answers, with the army, but couldn't think of any way to stop any of it. She couldn't save a single life, couldn't stop it at all.

CHAPTER FIFTEEN

As they headed south, Kevin saw the world burning, and he couldn't help the pain that came with that. The Hive were striking back against his world, and now it wouldn't be long before they destroyed it.

"I have seen this before," Ro said. "But I never understood the horror of it before now. I never truly understood what it *meant*."

Kevin could believe that. Within the emotionless cocoon of the Hive, the destruction of a world was just a matter of necessary steps and the inconvenience of resistance from so-called inferior beings. Here, now, with city ships hovering in the distance, striking down with every weapon they possessed, it was impossible not to see it as a horror that would never stop.

"They're destroying everything," Chloe said, and Kevin could hear the horror there. From the driver's seat of the skidder, Kevin could see the destruction of buildings, of public spaces, of everything that got in the aliens' way.

He could also see the people fighting back.

In a small town on the northern fringes of California, he saw ordinary men and women struggling with some of the Hive's controlled warriors, fighting back with guns and other weapons, throwing globes containing a blue substance that seemed to make the aliens rear back, fearful of contact with it in a way that those controlled by the Hive had never before been afraid of anything.

Those that it did strike seemed to collapse, and then rose up again, looking around in obvious confusion. Kevin saw them turn and then do the impossible: they started to fight back against the other aliens.

"A cure," he said. "They've found it!"

"They have," General s'Lara said. "And it may give them the chance that they need."

Then Kevin saw a group of alien ships closing in, getting ready to fire. One of the Purest stood on a golden disk, commanding the destruction from above in shining golden armor.

"We have to help," he said.

General s'Lara shook her head. "We can't, Kevin. You know that we can't. Sometimes, you have to focus on winning the war, not every—hey!"

She cried out as Ro pushed her from her skidder, her suit slowing her descent so that she landed with no more than a gentle tumble.

"I'm sorry, General," the former Purest called out, "but I *cannot* stand by while another of my kind commits these atrocities."

Ro shot toward the fighting, lifting the weapon that he held and firing at the aliens as he went. His skidder couldn't go as high as the Hive's ships, but it was still enough to get it close to the golden disk as he shot at it.

"We have to help him, Kevin!" Chloe called out.

Kevin was already accelerating toward the fight, weaving their vehicle toward the conflict across the landscape, and skidding around the edge of a set of buildings. He lost sight of Ro for a moment, and when he saw the alien again, he was struggling with the Purest on the golden platform.

They fought hand to hand with the same speed and beauty that Kevin had seen the last time Ro had fought one of his own kind. The two exchanged attacks with utter precision and ferocity, fighting back and forth while beneath them, the greater fight continued.

Then the Purest struck out with a blade of pure golden metal, knocking Ro down to one knee.

"Jump away, Ro!" Chloe called out, although at that distance it was impossible to know if the former Purest would be able to hear them. "Your suit will save you!"

It was the sensible thing to do. If Ro jumped, they would be able to get to him, and Kevin was sure that the Ilari would be able to find a way to heal him. Ro just needed to jump clear, or better yet, hold on until Kevin and Chloe could get there to help.

Kevin saw Ro look around, and for a moment, he thought the alien was looking their way. For an instant, just an instant, Kevin was sure that he felt some flicker of the connection the two had possessed when they had both been a part of the Hive.

Thank you both. I am free thanks to you. I die as myself! *I* choose *this!*

"No!" Kevin called out, but Ro was already forcing himself to his feet. The other Purest didn't hesitate, striking out with that golden sword, clutching Ro close as he thrust it up through his abdomen.

Then Kevin saw Ro grab back at the Purest, holding on tight and dragging the helmet from its head. The former member of the Hive pulled the helmet on even though the Purest struck out with the blade again, and again.

Below, every alien still under the control of the Hive froze in place, while ships started to tumble from the sky. It was everything that Kevin had managed on the Ilari's world and more. It was a moment of perfectly held peace, even as the Purest continued to thrust with that deadly blade. Below, Kevin could see the people there striking out, attacking the frozen aliens while they had the chance to do it.

Kevin ignored all of it, powering the skidder up toward the golden disc while Chloe fired her pistol at the golden figure again and again. Some of the shots hit, but they merely glanced from the armor. The golden figure turned to them, raising its sword aloft so that it crackled with power like a lightning bolt and letting Ro collapse.

Kevin knew it was about to fire at them, and when it did, they wouldn't be able to avoid it. That much power would blast their craft from the sky, and even if it didn't, it would probably punch straight through their shields.

Then Ro reached out, grabbing hold of the Purest again. Power crackled around both of them as he did it, seeming to flow over every surface of them. It was only as Ro took a step toward the edge of the disc that Kevin understood what his friend was about to do.

"No, please no," Kevin whispered.

Ro flung himself and the Purest from the disc to tumble down toward the world below. Ro tumbled clear of the Purest as he fell, floating as his suit tried to protect him, but Kevin could see that it was already too late for that. The Purest tumbled faster, crunching onto the ground, leaving it unmoving.

Kevin didn't care about the Purest. He only cared about getting to Ro.

He plunged the silvery skidder down toward the ground, and the spot where his friend had fallen. As soon as they were at ground level, Kevin jumped clear, and Chloe jumped with him, both ignoring the fighting that was continuing even now. The people there would have the advantage now, after all Ro had done, and out of the corner of his eye, Kevin could see the Ilari joining the fight. They fought from their skidders, firing from the back, striking out with deadly accuracy.

Kevin ignored it all as he went over to the fallen form of his friend. Kevin could already see that Ro was gone, his body too still, too limp, too *lifeless*.

"No!" Chloe said. "He can't be. He can't be dead."

For a moment, Kevin didn't know what to say, but then he remembered the words he'd heard across that brief moment of renewed connection with Ro.

"He said that he was free thanks to you," Kevin said. "He said that he chose this. He chose, Chloe."

He put a hand on her shoulder, not knowing how else to comfort her. Kevin could feel his own grief at the death of his friend, but he also knew that this was the biggest freedom Ro could have had: the freedom to save others instead of hurting them; the freedom to atone for the past.

He stood there with Chloe while around them, people started to gather. Some of them looked like former soldiers, some like scavengers, some like they were just ordinary people who had found themselves caught up in the violence. Even some of the aliens were standing around, clearly confused about what they were going to do next.

One man came forward, dressed in combat fatigues. "I don't know who you are, but you arriving like that changed the course of this. All of you," he added as General s'Lara and the Ilari started to touch down in the space around them.

"My name is Kevin," Kevin said. "This is Chloe, and General s'Lara, and…"

"Wait, Kevin?" the man said. "As in Luna's friend Kevin?" He stepped back from Kevin for a moment, staring at him. "It *is* you. My name's Mullins. I remember you from the Survivors' camp, and from the news. If you're back… Luna will want to see you."

"Luna?" Kevin said, unable to contain his sudden need to know. "Luna's alive, and safe, and—"

"I don't know about *safe*," Mullins said. "I think everywhere is a war right now. The quarry…"

"What quarry?" Kevin asked. "Where is Luna?"

Mullins looked over to the others there. "She sent us out from the quarry to tell people about the cure, and about how it could be used as a weapon, if the right energy is put through it."

"The right energy?" Chloe asked. Kevin could see the tears on her face, but she seemed to be ignoring them. Perhaps she was thinking about revenge.

"Enough energy causes a reaction with the mineral that forms the basis of the cure," Mullins said. "It bursts, and the energy wave… it's like a cure in itself."

General s'Lara looked thoughtful, and Kevin could definitely understand why.

"Energy can be arranged," she said, touching something on her suit so that one of the shields there flashed into visibility.

Kevin saw Mullins shake his head, though.

"It doesn't work like that. They… Barnaby tried to explain it. Something about having to tune the energy to what it's trying to affect. It needs *their* energy. We've been shooting lumps of it with their energy guns, or planting it where we know they'll fire. It lets us win battles in seconds."

Kevin could see the obvious problem with that, though, and it seemed that so could the general.

"Down here, but not against the city ships, or that world ship of theirs."

"Maybe Luna will have a better answer," Mullins said, although he didn't look happy.

"What is it?" Kevin asked.

The man sighed. "This is what it's like here, where we've just been gathering a little of the cure, but the quarry… it's one of the main sites for gathering it, and it's our base, and… Luna has an army now. Worse, we think we saw three city ships heading for LA."

"Three?" Kevin said. If that was where Luna still was, then she was in grave danger. The kind of danger that made his heart tighten in his chest. "Where is she?"

"There's a quarry near LA," Mullins said. "If you have a map, I'll show you."

General s'Lara touched something on her arm, and an image of the world appeared, obviously taken from sensors of some kind.

"Here," Mullins said. "We're here, and the quarry is… here."

It seemed so far to go, even then, but that just meant that there was no time to lose.

"Any people you have to spare," he said, "bring them to LA. That's where this will be fought and won."

"Or lost," Mullins said.

Kevin knew he was right, but he couldn't think about it like that. All that mattered was getting there. It was their best chance of winning all this; their best chance of actually finding enough of the mineral to make a difference.

Kevin got back on his skidder, and he was alone this time, because Chloe got on with General s'Lara, in the spot Ro had occupied. Kevin guessed it was the best way she had to feel close to him, so soon after he was gone. One by one, the Ilari mounted up, turning their vehicles toward the south again.

Kevin launched his forward, moving with all the speed that it had, and hoping that he would get there in time. He raced for LA, for the chance of winning this, but above all, for Luna.

CHAPTER SIXTEEN

Kevin raced for LA, pushing his skidder, and himself, as hard as he dared. Getting there was what mattered at this point; getting there in *time*. If they arrived, and the battle was already lost, Kevin wasn't sure if he would be able to live with it all. If something had happened to Luna...

"Kevin, we'll get there," Chloe called out from the back of General s'Lara's vehicle. "We'll be in time."

"Only if we hurry," Kevin replied. He was certain of it. Luna was in danger, and so was the whole world. If they didn't get to this battle soon, then it might be too late for everyone, and not just those in LA. The Hive would destroy the Earth, and once they had gotten rid of the one weapon that seemed to have a chance to stop them, they would go on to ravage the universe.

The best part about the skidders was that they weren't slowed down by the landscape. As fast as they were, it would have meant nothing if they had been slowed down at every step by the need to dodge around cars or pick safe routes across broken ground. Instead, Kevin could float forward just above it all, moving at the kind of speed that probably wasn't as great as any of the spaceships that he'd been in, but still felt faster than any of it.

He skimmed over streams and down the length of roads, so fast that the landscape flashed past, cities appearing and disappearing in the distance. Kevin thought they must be Sacramento, then San Francisco, then San Jose. Kevin could see the signs of violence coming from some of them, with ships firing down at the ground, and energy flashing up from fighters amongst the buildings.

Kevin wished they could stop and help, but General s'Lara had been right before: they needed to fight the battles that would actually win this war, or they would risk losing everything.

He forced the skidder forward again, looking around to check that the others were there. They were; General s'Lara and Chloe were next to him, while dozens of Ilari skidders flew behind, each carrying warriors who could fight as well as anyone Kevin had seen, despite their love for peace. He had to believe that it would be enough.

It was easier to believe that before Kevin saw the first glimpses of LA in the distance, though. Seeing the city there, with not one,

104

but three city-sized ships hovering above it, it was hard to believe that anything could prevail against so many enemies.

Each of the city ships was slightly different. One was almost perfectly circular, while another was closer to the shape of some giant ray, and the third was like a great rock hanging in the sky, smaller ships pouring from it like an avalanche.

They fired down at the city below, and at a spot just beyond it, the weapon blasts coming down like lightning from some great, impossible storm. Instinctively, Kevin knew that would be where Luna and her army were.

As he got closer, he could see the damage that the alien attacks were doing, with buildings collapsing, and great clouds of dust rising from every impact. Piece by piece, LA was being reduced to rubble, a skyline that had once been filled with tall buildings turned into something flat, unrisen.

Above it all, Kevin could see the world ship gathering together power, getting ready to fire down at the world and tear it apart. Just the sight of it made him think of the way the Ilari's world had been destroyed, one layer at a time, the atmosphere burning off, the water boiling, the plates on its surface cracking apart in the moments before it exploded.

"No," Kevin said. "I won't let that happen again. I won't."

They skirted LA, heading for the spot where Mullins had told them the quarry lay. Even if they hadn't had the precise spot marked on General s'Lara's sensor map, Kevin would still have been able to guess where it was. The battle around the city seemed to target one point there, the smaller ships converging on it, the larger ones firing down while energy fire came back from the ground.

Anyone sensible would have turned the other way and run, but Kevin knew that Luna was somewhere at the center of that fight. More than that, he knew that *this* was the fight that mattered. They *had* to be a part of this, or everything would soon be lost.

Ahead, two armies clashed, mingling together in the violence until there were places where it seemed impossible to tell which one was which. Ships darted low, and Kevin could see the damage they were doing as they strafed the battle, seemingly at random. The whole whirlpool of violence seemed to center on the quarry at its heart.

"Ready?" Kevin asked the others.

"We will engage the ships," General s'Lara said. "Then dive down to punch a hole in their defenses."

"We can do this," Chloe said. Very deliberately, she climbed back onto Kevin's skidder. "Someone has to make sure you're all right. I doubt Luna would forgive me if I let the aliens get to you before you found her again."

Kevin nodded. "Thank you. All of you. And if this is the last moment I see some of you, then…"

"Speeches afterwards," General s'Lara said. "*Winning* now."

Kevin forced the skidder forward, heading for the heart of the battle, his own gun cradled ready to use.

He and the Ilari hit it like a silver spear, slashing through the Hive's forces, firing down at the enemy without stopping, without coming close enough to get bogged down in them. Kevin lifted his gun one handed, firing down at a cluster of great beasts that seemed to be tearing into the humans there. He saw his shots strike home, while Chloe fired her pistol and whipped her shock baton round at one of the controlled who got too close.

Then they were clear, out in open space. They whipped around, and Kevin saw the Ilari shoot up toward a squadron of the Hive's ships as they tried to come in low to strafe the battle, leaping up like a shoal of flying fish, right to the limits of the skidders' range. Their pilots shot at the Hive ships from underneath, firing at their weak underbellies. Kevin saw a pair of the ships go down, the Ilari's weapons punching through vital spots. The rest kept going, firing down at the battle once again.

"Focus on the ground," General s'Lara called out to Kevin. "My people will deal with the ships. They need to *see* you, and you need to get to your friend, if you can."

Kevin and Chloe plunged into the battle for another pass, and another. They lanced through the mass of enemy troops, turning at the end of each pass, trying to work out which spots they would be able to help most in. That was harder and harder to judge as Luna's forces cured more and more of them, taking aliens from the control of their Hive masters.

Above them, Kevin saw one of the Ilari soldiers fall from the sky, then another, even though Hive ships crashed down around them. Worse, now the ships were pulling back, and even Kevin could see that the ships were out of range of the skidders as they rose into the sky.

General s'Lara pulled back close to him, falling into formation once again. "We can't reach them now. We have to rely on the energy cannons. At least most of their crews seem to have been converted back."

It wasn't enough and Kevin knew it. They had to find a way to do more. He pointed to another spot, where it seemed that the aliens had a group of the Survivors pinned down.

"There," he said. "We can at least help there."

General s'Lara nodded, and they plunged toward the battle once more. Kevin clutched his weapon, firing in short bursts as they plunged forward. Kevin saw Chloe shoot down target after target, while his own shots went into the great mass of attacking aliens, and he couldn't see the results.

They got closer and closer, skidding in close to the ranks of the Hive's soldiers, filled with aliens of every conceivable variety, from the black-armored soldiers Kevin had seen before, to creatures with far too many legs, and lizard-like beings with claws like knives.

He was still staring when something leapt up from the battle below toward the skidder.

The creature looked frog-like, but covered in living armor, and holding an energy rifle that crackled with power. Kevin had a moment to see it approaching, and then he found himself smashed from the skidder, tumbling from it toward the battle below. His suit slowed the fall enough that his bones didn't shatter on impact with the ground, but even so, the sheer speed that the skidder had been moving meant that it knocked the wind from him.

Kevin rolled onto his back and saw that the frog thing was already on its feet, weapon in its hand. It started to raise that gun, and Kevin rolled hard to one side, barely dodging as an energy bolt slammed into the ground where he had been. He rolled again, and another bolt barely missed him.

He saw his own gun a few feet away, but it might as well have been a thousand miles. The moment he moved, he was sure the alien would shoot him down. Even so, Kevin leapt, because standing there would be even worse. He felt something scrape across the shields of his suit, energy flaring so bright before his eyes that it all but blinded him. When he felt his hand connect with the gun where it lay in the dirt, he lifted it and fired at the spot where he hoped the frog thing would be.

As his vision cleared, he saw it standing there, staring down at the hole in its chest for the seconds it took before its brain realized that it was dead, and it collapsed onto the ground of the battlefield.

If the frog alien had been the only enemy, that would have been all of it, but now Kevin could see another dozen enemies around him, and none of them looked as though they had been changed back by the Survivors' cure. It seemed as though he'd landed in their lines, and now they were getting ready to fire, lifting weapons that Kevin was sure his shields wouldn't be able to withstand this time.

"Kevin!"

Kevin looked up at the sound of Chloe's voice above him. Their skidder was shooting in close to him, and Kevin knew what she intended. The only problem was that they would need to time this perfectly. He waited, and waited…

…and leapt.

His arms caught the slick metal of the vehicle, and he felt himself pulled up clear of the battle. He dragged himself back onto it, while Chloe drove them away from the main mass of the fighting.

She piloted it now, while Kevin did the shooting. He fired down into the mass of the aliens, trying to pick out the ones that represented the greatest danger to Luna's people. He shot at a massive ape thing, at an officer for some of the black-armored creatures, at a group of lizard men. Chloe darted the skidder in and out of the battle, while Kevin kept on firing.

It seemed to be working. The cure was making the battle on the ground better, converting the Hive's forces and turning them against those that were still in the fight. The Ilari's darting attacks slid into the body of the Hive's forces, and the human army on the ground held its position in spite of everything that was coming at it.

If the Hive hadn't had ships, it would have been simple.

It *did* have ships, though, and those fired down at the battle, seemingly at random. The Hive could afford to kill its own troops, because the ones who were still controlled would fight on regardless. Hive hunter ships swooped in, firing down again and again, even when energy blasts came up to target them.

It got worse when the city ships started to fire too.

Those fired blasts of energy that were enough to bring down buildings, the force of their impact spreading out in waves that rippled out over the battle, killing anything in their way. Kevin saw soldiers and alien beasts alike swept aside like pins in front of a bowling ball. As one of the blasts hit nearby, he felt Chloe having to fight to keep their skidder from flipping over or crashing, surfing the energy wave and letting it carry them across the battle.

"We can't win, can we?" Chloe asked.

"We have to," Kevin said, although he couldn't see how then. They were winning the battle on the ground, but already, he could see hundreds more small ships plunging down from the city ships, each one probably carrying a dozen or more alien soldiers.

The ships above were a bigger problem. They couldn't fight them, couldn't hope to beat them. At least, Kevin assumed that, until he saw a ripple in the one piece of sky he could see beyond all of the city ships, and silvery craft started to appear.

"The Ilari!" he said. "It's the rest of their fleet!"

It couldn't be all of it. The big ships that could hold thousands of civilians must have been left behind, because how could those move fast enough through space to arrive even now? No, what hung above was a collection of fighting craft, silvery and shark-like, which plunged toward the city ships, firing down on them with weapons that seemed to rip through even their bulk.

Kevin saw the moment when one fell. The giant, ray-like form of one of the city ships fractured like a dropped plate, fissures opening up in its form to let through the firepower of the Ilari fleet. Explosions rocked along it, and now it seemed to drift away from LA, creaking and tearing as it broke into fragments that fell from the sky in a rain of alien metal and living rock. Where the pieces hit, Kevin saw explosions on a scale that could have wiped out a small town.

The Ilari didn't have it all their own way though. Far above him, Kevin saw a ship blasted into silvery dust by fire from Hive ships, while their fighters quickly moved up to combat the Ilari ships. The Ilari shot down far more of the Hive's ships than they lost, but they had far fewer ships to start with. It was far too evenly poised for Kevin's liking.

At least it meant that the battle wasn't being strafed by ships that they couldn't fight back against. Now it was just the seemingly endless cascade of troop ships, dropping alien after alien onto the battlefield. Kevin kept up his fire, seeing General s'Lara and the others darting in and out of the pockets of fighting, firing down at groups of the Hive's creatures and then hurrying away before they fought back.

Not all of them made it. Some of them fell under alien fire; others found themselves dragged into ground-level fights with far too many of the Hive's soldiers. For Kevin, it felt as though the battle was poised on a knife edge.

General s'Lara beckoned him over.

"I need to hold things here," she said. "We need that weapon, Kevin. We need a way to win this, or the Hive will wear us down, just as they did on our worlds. You need to go find this girl of yours, Luna."

Kevin didn't like the idea of going. It felt too much like running away. It felt as though he were abandoning his friends to die while he got to safety.

"You need to go, Kevin," Chloe said, as if guessing what he was thinking.

"I need to go?" Kevin echoed. "What about you?"

Chloe guided their skidder as close to General s'Lara's craft as possible, and then leapt over with the lightness that her augmented body gave her.

"I'm going to help here," she said. "I'm going to kill as many of them as I can, and keep them off until you can save us all. You can *do* this, Kevin."

Kevin wanted to argue, wanted to call her back, but General s'Lara and Chloe were already flying away, heading into the thick of the battle. A part of him wanted to follow, wanted to try to help, but he knew that there was only one way to help right then. He needed to do what General s'Lara and Chloe wanted him to do—he needed to find the weapon that the Survivors had come up with, and find a way to win this for good.

Looking out, Kevin could see that the battle was still at its thickest close to the quarry. Getting through it wouldn't be easy, but he knew that he needed to. He needed to find the weapon. He needed to finish this.

He needed to get to Luna, whatever it took.

CHAPTER SEVENTEEN

Kevin was determined as he guided his skidder toward the quarry, the battle flashing past beneath him. Energy fire came up at him, and he wove the vehicle left and right, trying to avoid the worse of it. Some of it flickered off his shields even then, while more washed off the skidder's silver surface.

Kevin kept going, not even bothering to fire down in response. It didn't matter now whether he killed one enemy or a hundred; all that mattered was getting to the quarry, and to Luna. He kept his head down and powered the skidder forward, hoping that its sheer speed would carry it past the danger.

It didn't.

Kevin felt the moment when the energy blast hit the skidder full on, slamming into it and sending sparks crackling across it. The skidder tilted to the side, flipping over like a surfboard that had caught a wave at the wrong angle. Kevin could see a hole punched through it, and it took him a moment to realize that he was seeing it from several feet away.

He was falling, and only the effects of his suit slowed the fall enough that it wouldn't be fatal. Kevin remembered to tuck and roll this time, spinning over the hard ground around the quarry while somewhere a little further off, the skidder crashed into the ranks of the enemy's forces. Kevin heard the thud of the explosion, and felt the wash of heat from it.

He was already up, his energy gun in his hands, running for the Survivors' lines, and the quarry beyond. He couldn't stay and fight all the Hive's troops, but he could get past them, get through them and continue. Kevin fired as an armored Hive soldier stepped in front of him, bringing it down without stopping, Then dodged to one side as a mantis-like creature with blades for arms darted into the space he had just occupied. Kevin kept moving, not slowing even for an instant.

"We see you, Kevin McKenzie," voices hissed around him in unison, speaking from a dozen throats at once. "You cannot escape the Hive. We will bring you back to us, and make you a part of us once more. You will give us more worlds. You cannot avoid this."

Hands turned in toward him, some grabbing, some holding weapons and apparently trying to kill. Kevin threw himself flat as energy fire went over his head, rolled back to his feet, and shot back as two large, beetle-like creatures ran at him.

Step by sprinting step, Kevin made his way toward the quarry. He felt as though it stood a hundred miles away, but in reality, it was probably only that many yards. He fired ahead of him, trying to aim at the spots where the Hive's creatures looked as though they were the most dangerous, trying to cut a path through the chaos of the battle.

It was anything but easy. Around him, people and aliens fought, and fired, and sometimes leapt for cover. All the while, Kevin kept his eyes open, looking out for any sign of Survivors he knew, or better yet, of Luna.

He saw Bobby before he saw Luna, barking around the edges of a thick knot of Hive troops who were firing from the cover of a cluster of rocks. They had a group of humans pinned down a little way away, near the entrance to the quarry.

A second later, and Kevin saw Luna for the first time since he'd left Earth. She was there amid the group of human fighters, firing back at the aliens and shouting orders that it seemed that everyone rushed to obey. Right now, though, it seemed that the Hive's soldiers fired every time she dared to stick her head out from cover. Several of them were slowly working to flank her cluster of fighters, moving around so that they would have a clear line of fire from which to pick them off.

Kevin didn't hesitate. He ran forward with a cry, firing at the Hive soldiers who were pinning Luna and the others in place. Firing from this angle, he was able to catch them almost from behind, shooting down a couple before they could even start to react. Others turned toward him, returning fire, and Kevin leapt to the side, hunkering down in a section of grass while he fired.

The distraction seemed to be enough for Luna and her troops to act. Even as the aliens fired at him, he saw Luna spring from her cover, shooting down one of the enemies who had been trying to flank her. The others with her brought down more, and now, Kevin was able to open fire again, trapping the last of them in the crossfire.

Most of the Survivors were standing there looking relieved that they had survived the firefight, but Luna ran forward, throwing her arms around him.

"Kevin! You're alive!"

"And you're cured," he managed in response, barely able to believe it. "How? What happened?"

Luna might have started to say something to that, but Bobby chose that moment to jump up at them, almost knocking them both over.

"Yes," Kevin said to the dog, as Bobby wagged his tail frantically. "I'm happy to see you too."

He was *more* than happy to see Luna. He thought that he'd lost her forever. He thought that he would never have a chance to tell her everything that he felt about her. Kevin couldn't stand that thought, so he opened his mouth to tell her exactly that…

But an explosion nearby cut him off, shaking the ground beneath his feet.

"Maybe we should do this inside the quarry?" Luna suggested, and Kevin could only nod, almost deaf from the boom of the impact.

She led the way, back past a defensive line from which members of the Survivors fired out with rifles and energy weapons, machine guns, and even a rocket launcher. Kevin had no idea where they'd managed to get all of that weaponry, but he was grateful they had, because at least it meant that they could put a dent in the Hive's attempts to attack the quarry.

"We should be safe here for a little while," Luna said. "But we only have a little bit of time. The battle is too close."

Kevin had seen that. The whole thing felt poised, and unless they found some way to change things, Kevin had a horrible feeling that the Hive would win eventually. For now, though, there was only Luna, and the brief moment of safety when they could talk.

"How did you get back?" Luna asked. "Where's Chloe?"

"We…" Kevin shook his head, not knowing where to even begin when it came to telling Luna everything that had happened. "The Hive took us for a while, and they made me a part of it, but we escaped. Another group of aliens too us in, and they brought us back to Earth."

"They're the ones on the surfboard things?" Luna asked. "They're the ones having *that* battle?"

She pointed up, to where the Ilari fleet was still engaged in a vicious conflict with the Hive's forces. Ilari ships fired energy beams and rippled with shields, destroying smaller Hive ships with ease. There always seemed to be more of them, though, and even as Kevin watched, he saw another of the Ilari vessels reduced to silvery dust. He didn't want to think about how many of the aliens would have been aboard.

"They're… incredible. They look as though they could almost beat the others."

Kevin nodded. "Their leader is General s'Lara. They all have their own AIs, and they know things about shields and weapons and things that almost no one else does. The Hive still managed to destroy their world, though."

"How?" Luna asked.

"They used me."

Luna didn't say anything, just threw her arms around Kevin, and he knew that she would know exactly how guilty he would feel, and how easily the image of it flashed through his mind whenever he closed his eyes.

"We'll stop them," Luna said. "We have a weapon: the mineral… Do you know about the mineral?"

"The one that can break the Hive's control when you put energy through it?" Kevin said. Luna nodded. "One of your people told us about it."

"Did he tell you that it's not enough?" Luna asked. She looked around the battle deliberately. "We can sit in the quarry, and they don't dare to fire on it because of the blast it will cause, and we can transform any aliens they send at us on the ground…"

"But they just keep coming," Kevin said. He knew how the Hive worked. It didn't care about its troops. It would just keep sending controlled creatures until it overwhelmed the fighters below, or until its world ship could fire down from above and destroy everything. "And… and you can't deal with the ships."

"Exactly," Luna said. "We can't use the mineral against them. We can't do anything about *that*." Kevin saw her point to the world ship above.

"Can I see the mineral?" he asked.

Luna nodded. "If we're quick. The others know what they're doing, but they will need to see me. A lot of them say they are only fighting because I'm there."

"Trust you to start off controlled, and end up with an army," Kevin said, with a smile that was mostly about the fact that Luna was safe, and free, and still the same old Luna. He loved that about her, but then, he loved everything about her.

Luna led the way down into the quarry, to where pile after pile of blue-tinged mineral sat waiting.

"We know what it can do," she said, "and we know how to process it to make a cure. We even know that firing on it with the Hive's weapons will make a blast that will disrupt any of their controlled aliens around it, but we don't know how to make it work on a large scale."

"What's the problem?" Kevin asked. There was so much of the mineral here that it seemed as though it would be easy to convert the Hive's entire army.

"We have a couple of people who have worked this out," Luna said. "You remember Barnaby?"

Kevin nodded. From what he remembered, the boy had been as clever as anyone he'd met. He'd been able to help them find the first potential cure when no one else could.

"What have they worked out?" Kevin asked.

"There are three elements to this weapon," Luna said. She gestured to the piles of minerals waiting there. "The mineral is the first one, reacting like that. It's the one we have."

"And the other two?" Kevin asked. The mineral looked impressive enough as it was, but it also seemed still and inert. It wasn't giving off any sign of the power that Luna claimed it possessed.

"The second part is energy," Luna said. "We had a battle by the place where we found the mineral, and when the alien energy bolts came close, it glowed. I… I managed to put it where they would shoot, and it exploded. It converted the controlled."

"If it's just a question of energy," Kevin said, "the Ilari can produce all the power you need. They have energy cannons and shields, and…"

He saw Luna shake her head, and it was enough to make him trail off.

"It's not enough," Luna said. "The energy… it's like it vibrates at a specific frequency. If we hit the mineral with the aliens' weapons, it works, but nothing else seems to. Barnaby sad something about it vibrating at the right frequency to affect the nanites they use to control people."

That was enough to make hope rise up in Kevin's chest. If they could genuinely disrupt the source of the connections that formed the Hive, then this might be enough to do everything they had hoped. It might actually be enough to win the war, not just the battle in front of them.

"So how do we use it?" Kevin said.

"That's the problem," Luna said. "We can throw lumps of it and hit them with shots from their rifles. We can put bigger pieces of it in places we think they'll shoot." She shook her head. "It's not enough."

No, Kevin thought, it wasn't. It meant either targeting a few of the Hive at a time, or waiting and hoping that they made a big mistake. Either way, it wasn't going to do anything about the world ship, or the battle in the sky, or any of the parts of this that *mattered* to the world. To do that, they would have to find a way to change the way the mineral reacted, or somehow tune an energy signal to the frequency it required, or…

"I have an idea," Kevin said. He patted his suit, trying to find if it had an inbuilt communicator. "General s'Lara?"

It took him a couple of attempts before the suit's AI got the message, and the general's voice came through in his ear.

"Kevin?"

"General, we need your help back at the quarry. They have a weapon there, but we need things to make it work."

"What things?" the general asked.

"We need energy, and we need to be able to tune that energy to a specific frequency," Kevin said.

"We can provide all the energy you need," the general said. "Would an energy cannon from one of the ships be enough?"

"Only if we can tune it," Kevin said. "And I'm pretty sure that the Hive has defenses against energy blasts. What we need is some kind of signal that can get through what they have and…"

Now an idea came to him. It wasn't a good idea. It certainly wasn't a safe one. Even so, he couldn't think of a better way to do things. The more he thought about it, the more certain he was. This was what he was meant for.

"You've thought of something, haven't you?" Luna said.

"I… think so," Kevin said.

He explained his idea to them. It didn't take long. Kevin watched Luna's face while he did it, and he could see the worry there, the fear.

"No," she said, "you can't."

"I *have* to," Kevin said.

"No, I won't let you," Luna said.

Kevin shook his head. "I'm not a part of your army, Luna."

"But you're my…" Luna paused, as if she couldn't find the words.

Kevin put a hand on her shoulder. "I know. This is the only way though."

"I…" She threw her arms around him.

Kevin didn't say goodbye, but they both knew that it might be. There were so many things that he wanted to say to her then, so many moments that he wished he could share. All he could do, though, was hold her close, wishing that he never had to let her go.

Finally, there was nothing to do but pull back.

"General s'Lara, do you know what you have to do?" he asked.

"I believe so," the general replied.

This was it then—the moment when he had to actually do this; the moment that he'd been heading toward since the very start of all of this. Kevin wasn't sure what the odds of surviving this were, but he suspected that they weren't very good at all.

He held onto Luna briefly, and her grip was so tight that when he pulled back, it was hard to do it. Or maybe it was just that he didn't *want* to let go of her. Then it was time, and he pulled away, heading for the center of the quarry. Above, the world ship continued to glow, building up the power to tear the Earth apart.

He had to hope that this would work, or the whole world would die.

CHAPTER EIGHTEEN

Kevin sat at the controls of a small Ilari ship, staring up at the Hive world ship as it got bigger and bigger, trying to ignore the fear of everything that might happen next. Chloe sat beside him, looking strangely calm considering that they were both going back toward the place that had done them so much harm before.

"You didn't have to come for this," Kevin said.

"Yes I did," Chloe said, as if he were being stupid by even suggesting that she could have stayed behind. She flexed the altered arm that the Hive had given her. "Yes, I did."

"Okay," Kevin said. His hands brushed over the controls, but didn't really do anything. This was an Ilari craft after all, and the AI controlling it was more than capable of flying a simple course like this. Around them, more ships flew in formation, unoccupied except for more of the mineral, moving close to the world ship as one.

"You realize that there's a chance they might just shoot us out of the sky as we get closer?" Kevin said. "This might not work. I need to be on the world ship for this, but—"

"And I need to be there to make sure that you get out okay," Chloe insisted. "Luna won't forgive me if I don't bring you back to her."

"I wouldn't have thought you would care what a cheerleader thought," Kevin said, thinking back to what Chloe always used to call Luna. She'd meant that Luna seemed like she had a perfect, cared for life where nothing bad ever happened. Kevin guessed that things had changed for them all since then.

"Yes, well, we've all been through a lot," Chloe said. She looked over at him. "She loves you, Kevin, and it's obvious you love her. You need to let her know that when you get back."

She made it all sound so easy. Then again, Kevin guessed that compared to fighting off an alien invasion, practically anything counted as easy. As he looked across at her, Chloe seemed determined, and more focused than she had since they first met. He guessed that this had changed all of them. If somehow they came through this, the whole world would need to start to adjust to everything that had happened to it.

First, though, they needed to find a way to get through this.

"They won't shoot us down," Chloe said. She sounded as though she wanted to believe it. "They won't shoot us down."

"Not with the mineral aboard," Kevin said. Not with them there either. The Hive had been trying to recapture him in the battle, and had been seeking out the mineral that they carried when they came to Earth. Between the two, he had to believe that the Hive would want to let them land.

He wanted to believe it, but that didn't mean it was certain. They could still shoot the ship down. They could still decide to kill him and Chloe, and there would be nothing either of them could do.

Slowly, little by little, the world ship grew closer, an aperture on its barren surface open to receive them. Kevin felt a slight jolt, and the ship's engines whined, then a synthesized voice filled the ship's interior.

"The ship has been controlled by a gravity ray," the voice said. "We have decided to allow it to avoid engine overload, and because it is where we are going anyway."

Their ship floated toward the waiting mouth of the world, coming up into a space that was far too familiar as the endless city of the interior came into view. Kevin had been in this space before. He recognized the factory districts below, and the vat-filled spaces, the tenements, and, beyond it all, the golden spire.

The ship flew in a straight line toward the square in front of the tower, touching down as delicately as if it had been placed there by a giant hand. Around the ship, Kevin could see at least a dozen of the Purest standing there, all wearing their golden armor and carrying the weapons that seemed so devastating in their hands.

Kevin heard the engines shut off and he stood, moving with Chloe to the main doors.

"Are you ready?" Kevin asked her.

Chloe shook her head. "No, but we're going to have to do it anyway, aren't we?"

"Yes," Kevin said. He activated the door and stepped out.

The weight of pressing gravity hit him and Chloe at the same moment, squashing them flat. But they had felt this before, and Kevin didn't fight it. He knew it wouldn't do any good. Besides, he'd been half expecting it.

"Bring them up," Purest Lux called from the heart of the group there. The alien stood in light golden scales that formed a kind of robe, leaning on a staff that seemed to snap and sizzle with potential power.

Kevin and Chloe found themselves led forward, permitted to walk across the open square. Above, Kevin could see the great weapon of the world ship crackling with power, far closer to being able to fire than Kevin might have thought. It looked as if it was only hours, days at most, from destroying the Earth.

"So, you brought whole shiploads of the substance," Purest Lux said. "You were no doubt hoping that we would fire on you? Your friend has made good use of that tactic in her irrelevant little war."

"If it's so irrelevant," Kevin said, "why are you bothering to fight it?"

Purest Lux seemed to consider him for a moment or two. "There were those of the Purest who wished to fight, while complete control of a world always makes dissecting it easier."

The alien said that without a flicker of recognition regarding the lives that might be ruined by that "dissection."

"If you want the rest of the mineral," Kevin said, "you'll have to go out onto the surface to collect it. The landers are spread out around your world."

"A petty move," Purest Lux said. "Unless… do you hope that the Ilari ships can self-destruct to trigger the mineral? Our world is stronger than that, and the Hive's link will not be severed by *their* energy. You have come here for nothing, Kevin McKenzie. You have *failed.*"

Kevin shook his head. "I came to give you a chance. This can still end without the Hive being destroyed. Take your people and go. Withdraw from Earth. Give us back our planet, and every single thing you have taken, and you'll get to walk away from this."

"Such arrogance!" Purest Lux said, looking around at the other members of the Purest standing there. "Do you think that you can come here and give commands? Do you think that you can come here and demand that we act this way or that? Give me one good reason why I shouldn't blast you from existence, human."

He lifted his energy staff, and it was far too similar to the blade that had struck down Ro. For a moment, all Kevin could do was stare at it, but he knew that if he only did that, then Purest Lux *would* kill him.

"I think I'm too valuable to you for that," Kevin said. "After all, you've sent people after me down there whenever you've spotted me, haven't you? You still want me, and what I can do."

"So that is what this is?" Purest Lux said. "An attempt to bribe us to leave your planet alone? What is it that you offer? You, and the girl, and the goods you have brought in exchange for us leaving the Earth be?"

"Would it work?" Kevin asked, because if it truly would, then maybe he would even consider it. He might let them take him if it would avoid more death, and destruction, and worse.

"You cannot bargain when you have already brought everything with you," Purest Lux said. "I think we will just take you both, and the things you have brought, and still destroy your world."

He waved a slender hand, and the other Purest moved forward, grabbing Kevin and Chloe. Chloe fought back, kicking one away, but with so many of them there, it was impossible for her to do more than that. They grabbed her arms, pinning them in place.

They held Kevin too, all but carrying him as they moved together up into the golden tower. Kevin knew without having to ask where they were heading for.

"If you make me a part of the Hive again, you'll be destroyed," he promised.

Purest Lux laughed at that. "We are the Hive. We will not be intimidated. We do not know fear."

No, they didn't. Kevin had been counting on that.

They hauled him and Chloe up through the tower, up toward the room where they had been imprisoned before. The same machinery was there, the same screens showing views out over the Earth. Kevin had the feeling that the similarity was more than coincidence.

"You will return to being a part of the Hive," Purest Lux said. "The girl will be dissected to see how she managed to corrupt one of our number. Things will be as they should have been from the start."

"This is your last chance," Kevin said.

"Enough stalling," Purest Lux replied. "Bring him. Convert him."

They dragged Kevin to the machines. He fought against it, but only because he could remember what it had been like when the Hive had gone through his thoughts before. He could remember the pain, and that made Kevin fight back while they dragged him into place and fixed living, pulsing connectors to his head.

The pain was unbearable, or it would have been if Kevin had not been used to being in pain. He'd lived his life in it, had to fight through it every time his illness had struck at him. After the pain came the sensation of the Hive somewhere beyond, all those connections stretching out so that Kevin could feel the way it all fit together. He could feel the energy of the nanites that connected the

Hive starting to vibrate through him, and he could feel the frequency of that vibration as surely as he had ever felt any signal.

In that moment, Kevin knew that this was the moment he'd been living his whole life for. Everything had brought him to this. Without his illness, he wouldn't have been strong enough to do this. Without his gift, he wouldn't have been able to do any of what he did next.

"Now," Kevin said, into the communicator of his suit.

The Ilari signal came through it, vibrating through Kevin, and he grasped it as it came into him, matching it to the signal that he felt from the Hive in conjunction with the suit's AI. Kevin could see the two signals, the Hive's and the Ilari's, and he watched and watched until the two started to overlap.

"Almost there," Kevin managed. "Almost…" He saw the two overlap perfectly. "*Now!*"

His suit vibrated with the signal, its shields relaying it perfectly, pumping it out into the Hive's world ship. This, *this*, was what Kevin was for—the last piece of the weapon, the sight needed to aim it precisely. He did, and he felt the Hive's grip start to melt away.

"What is *happening*?" Purest Lux demanded, and Kevin could hear the emotion in the alien's tone now.

Kevin could feel the spread of the effect now. It rippled out in explosions at a frequency that no human would be able to hear. Those explosions did damage, ripping into the world ship at points that the Ilari had calculated, but their real effects came as Kevin felt creature after creature torn free from the control of the Hive. He felt their emotions coming through, felt each consciousness pass back to itself.

He even felt the Purest as emotions rushed into them, and that was the point where Kevin stood up, pulling the connectors from himself now that they couldn't hold him down any longer.

Around him, the Purest were pulling back, recoiling from the emotions that roiled through them. Kevin saw one on the ground, crying, while another was pressed back against the wall, hands out as if to ward off some kind of enemy.

"No, no, I didn't mean to, I couldn't…"

On the edge of the room, two more of the Purest seemed to be working screens, and those started to show riots in the streets of the world ship, creatures running in every direction, and violence breaking out as some of the more feral ones fell on others, and crowds started to gather around the golden spires.

Others headed for ships as alarms started to sound around the world ship.

"What have you done?" Purest Lux demanded. "What have you *done*?"

"What one of you should have done centuries ago," Kevin said. "I've picked apart the Hive. I've taken the thing you thought you didn't need, and given it back to you. How *do* those emotions feel?"

"It's overwhelming, isn't it?" Chloe said. "All those emotions flooding in; it's hard to cope with. Ro could have taught you how to deal with it all, but you *killed him*."

"I'll kill you!" Purest Lux said, lifting the energy staff. Power crackled out from it, and Kevin knew that there would be no way to dodge or avoid it. Not this close, and not with the effects of the connection to the Hive still so fresh.

Then a golden-armored figure threw itself between them, the flickering energy slamming into its armor and sending it sprawling to the wall.

"Why?" Purest Lux demanded, shouting it at the Purest who had just sacrificed itself to save Kevin's life.

"Because what we are doing… is evil," the Purest said. "Because… we need to… stop this…"

It collapsed back, and Kevin saw Purest Lux standing there, the energy staff still held ready.

"No," Purest Lux said, looking toward Kevin in obvious anguish. "No, you don't understand what you have *done*."

"I've given you back emotions," Kevin said. "I've given you empathy. I've let you see what you've done wrong."

"Wrong is what hurts the Hive!" Purest Lux screamed. "Right is making us strong! Emotions nearly destroyed us before, with their weakness, and their impulsiveness, and their blind rage. We must act calmly. We must act *together*."

Kevin looked around pointedly at the Purest who were still being overwhelmed by their emotions, and at the scenes of chaos slowly spreading across the world ship. Now, it seemed that more and more of the creatures there were heading for the Hive's ships. It didn't look like an invasion to Kevin so much as an evacuation; a world's worth of creatures heading out into space in the hope of somewhere better, having their freedom, but nothing else.

"No," Purest Lux said. "No, I will not allow it. We worked so hard to bring the Hive together. To stop the wars! To make us great! I will not allow it."

"Too late," Chloe said, beside Kevin, obviously enjoying the moment.

Purest Lux gestured, and in an instant, they were both flattened to the floor by increased gravity. It only took a moment for another of the Purest to release them, but by then, Purest Lux was already running.

"I will not allow this!" Purest Lux called out. "The Hive will be saved, and the chaos of Earth will be destroyed!"

CHAPTER NINETEEN

Kevin and Chloe chased Purest Lux through the golden tower, seeing the flash of light from the golden armor as they tried to keep up. Kevin was a little surprised that, despite how old Purest Lux looked compared to the other Purest of the Hive, he and Chloe were still having to run flat out to keep the alien in sight.

"It must be heading for the weapon," Chloe said.

Kevin nodded. He could see the glow of the world ship's weapon beyond, still charging, ready for its strike against Earth. Was it fully charged yet? Kevin didn't know, but he wasn't sure if it even mattered. If the energy beam just cracked the surface of the planet and burned its atmosphere rather than tearing it apart completely, that wasn't any better. It might not let the Hive harvest minerals from the Earth's interior, but it would still kill everyone down on its surface.

"We have to get there first!" Kevin called out.

The two of them kept running through the golden spire. They passed the fallen body of a guard, obviously brought down in the violence that had started in the wake of the Hive's control. Kevin stooped as he ran, snatching up the creature's energy weapon and firing after the retreating form of Purest Lux. The energy bolts flew off the walls.

They seemed to be catching up now, but ahead, they saw Purest Lux on a patch of ground that Kevin recognized. It touched its arm, and now one of the golden discs rose into the air, speeding out through an opening in the spire's wall.

"It's getting away," Kevin said, but Chloe looked determined.

"Not yet." She lifted her altered arm and squinted in concentration while she pressed something there. Another of the discs rose, and they hopped on it together.

They shot after the receding figure of Purest Lux, out through the city, sliding beneath an upside down walkway, then banking around a post that seemed to have been made from living flesh.

Below them, Kevin could see the world ship emptying. Creatures were still fighting in the streets as they were freed from the Hive's control, but now they seemed to be fighting to get away as much as to get revenge on the system that had controlled them. A few golden-armored figures appeared to be fighting back against them here and there, accompanied by those creatures who were too used to obeying to do anything else. They were too few, though, and the creatures around them quickly started to overwhelm them, simply trampling them in the rush to get clear of the Hive.

"The city ships are breaking away," Kevin said, pointing as below, several of those city-sized vessels that had remained as part of the world ship were breaking away from it, leaving shield-covered gaps out into space.

"Trying to concentrate," Chloe said as they zipped around more of the world ship's structures. Purest Lux was taking a weaving path ahead of them, through conduits and around large structures. Winged creatures flew past, ignoring all of them as they moved toward the waiting fleets of ships, obviously trying to find a way out of there.

"Left!" Kevin yelled as he saw Purest Lux lift the energy staff and aim it in their direction. He felt the golden disc jerk as Chloe wrenched it to one side, a bolt of energy rippling past to slam into a building behind them. It smashed a hole in the building, leaving fragments of metal and living building materials tumbling down.

More bolts of energy flickered past them, but now Chloe was trying to dodge, and they missed, again and again. The energy got close, but every twist and turn they took sent it past them to burst on the city around them.

"Fire back!" Chloe shouted out, while she continued to pilot the disc.

It took Kevin a moment to realize that he was just standing there, watching the progress of their chase, when he was still holding the energy rifle that he'd taken from the fallen guard.

He lifted it and started to fire, aiming for Purest Lux's retreating form. If the alien had been truly trying to flee, Kevin might have felt bad about firing at it from behind like that, but if they didn't find a way to stop Purest Lux then the Earth was doomed. He fired again and again, the shots cascading off the surfaces of the Hive's ship.

"Too close!" Chloe shouted as a bolt grazed the outer edge of their disc. It tumbled in the air for a moment, and Kevin could see the strain on Chloe's face as she righted it, but eventually they were flying level again, and Kevin kept firing at Purest Lux.

Some shots came up from the ground. Kevin couldn't work out if they were aimed at him and Chloe, at the now hated form of a Purest above the city, or just generally at the sight of golden discs.

There weren't many of the aliens down there to do it now. The world ship seemed to be emptying with frightening speed, leaving behind the shell of a world. It was a shell with cracks, too, because

Kevin could see the spots where the Ilari craft had exploded, laden with the mineral that had amplified the blast and turned it into something more. Fissures spread across the surface of the world ship, as the Ilari's AIs had calculated that they might, but Kevin knew that if the Hive had enough creatures working to repair it, they eventually would.

With so many of them leaving the ship, Kevin knew that would never happen. The best that would happen to the world ship now was that it would limp away so that the Hive could abandon it in favor of another place. Their time using it to pick worlds clean was over.

The two golden discs flashed through the interior of the world ship, locked in a chase that was only made more difficult because they all knew where it ended. The glow of the weapon ahead of them felt like a beacon, shining out and drawing them in toward it. It was the spot Purest Lux needed to get to, and the place Kevin and Chloe needed to reach first.

As they approached, Kevin kept firing, but now he was more careful with his shots, because he wasn't sure what would happen if the blasts struck the gathered energy of the weapon. It seemed to crackle there in the heart of the world ship, powerful as a sun even though it was compressed into a fraction of the space.

There was a kind of walkway around the weapon that probably served as a combination observation platform, command center, and spot from which to maintain the world ship's heart. At first, it didn't seem very large, but as Kevin got closer, he realized that it was just distance that had made it seem that way. Instead, the platform was broad enough that it could have held an entire choir of the aliens, there to witness the destruction of whatever world it was aimed at.

Kevin could see the Earth below, visible through a great aperture in the wall of the world ship, filling the whole of that space as if it sat in the crosshairs of some giant rifle sight. It did, when Kevin thought about it like that. The only question was whether they could do anything to prevent that weapon from firing and destroying everything.

"He's getting ready to land," Chloe said, bringing the golden disc around.

Purest Lux was indeed circling lower. The golden disc skidded in toward the platform, moving slower as it approached. Kevin risked another shot at the Hive's leader, but the alien fired back, and they barely banked away in time to avoid the energy blast. They moved in close now, their disc slowing in turn as they landed.

Purest Lux was ahead of them, standing at a console whose surface changed color in response to the movement of its hands. Its energy staff stood beside it, leaning against the console while it worked on the weapon's controls. The alien spun toward them as they advanced, and Kevin raised his gun in response.

"That's enough," Kevin said. "Step away from the controls, or you're dead."

"Then why not shoot me now?" Purest Lux demanded. "If you had the strength that comes from freedom from emotion, you would have done it by now."

"I'll do it," Kevin said. "Move, and I'll do it."

"What's wrong, boy?" Purest Lux asked. "Finding it hard to kill? Finding it hard to do what must be done? *That* is the weakness that comes from emotions."

"You don't seem to be having any problems with it," Chloe observed. "You're not a part of the Hive anymore, but you still want to destroy the Earth. What's *wrong* with you?"

"Wrong?" Purest Lux shot back. "Wrong is what harms my kind! I will not let you stop this. The Hive will be saved!"

It started to reach for its energy staff, and Kevin fired close to it. The blast skittered off the platform, making Purest Lux pull back sharply.

"The Hive *has* been saved," Kevin said. "All the people you've controlled for so long have been freed. They're abandoning your ship. You won't control them anymore."

"Freed?" Purest Lux shot back. "Chaos isn't *freedom*. It's destruction."

"The only thing I want to destroy right now is you," Chloe said, and she started forward toward Purest Lux before Kevin could tell her not to. Kevin could hear the anger in her voice as she kept going.

"You've hurt so many people," Chloe said, jabbing one hand into Purest Lux's armored chest. Her increased strength meant that the push forced the Purest to take a step back. She pushed out again. "Kevin might not be able to kill you, but I—"

She didn't get a chance to finish that as Purest Lux grabbed her and spun her round, snatching up its energy staff and holding it across her throat.

"This is what emotions do to you," Purest Lux said. "They make you weak. They leave you vulnerable. Look at the boy. He won't shoot, because that would risk shooting through you. Now, we're going back to the controls."

Kevin could only watch as Purest Lux dragged Chloe back toward the controls it had been working on. The Purest held her there with one arm and the staff, while the other started to work the controls, raising the hum of the energy weapon crackling overhead. Kevin saw Chloe struggling against that grip, but it seemed that Purest Lux was a lot stronger than its slender frame would suggest.

"Do it, Kevin!" Chloe called out, and Kevin knew what she had to mean. He didn't know if he could though. Luna might be the one he loved, but that didn't mean that he could just risk the life of a friend he had spent so long traveling with, and been through so much alongside. He aimed down the sights of his borrowed energy gun, Purest Lux's skull weaving in and out of focus.

Purest Lux laughed. "You think Kevin will do anything? It is the curse of the weak that they hesitate. They stand paralyzed when they should be acting. How does it feel, boy? How does it feel to know that the weapon is primed, and that with just one more touch, your world will be—"

Kevin took a deep breath, held it, and pulled the trigger.

The energy blast caught Purest Lux on the shoulder, spinning the alien around and leaving it facing Kevin, its grip on Chloe broken. It still had a grip on its energy staff, though, starting to raise it in spite of the burn marks that spread across its golden armor. Kevin knew that the moment it was level with him, the weapon would fire, and he struggled to bring his own up faster.

Chloe was quicker still, stepping forward and kicking Purest Lux in the chest as if she were kicking in a door. The impact carried the alien to the edge of the platform on which they stood, and then, with a shriek, Purest Lux fell over it.

Kevin could only watch as the Purest fell improbably, impossibly upward, toward the energy weapon at the heart of the Hive's world ship. Its energy staff was still clutched in its hands, and Kevin had to throw himself to one side as shot after shot rained down, slamming into the platform on which they stood.

Then Purest Lux slammed into the ball of energy poised to slam down into the Earth, and the alien's last cry echoed through the interior of the Hive ship, then it burst apart, the energy consuming it completely.

"It's over," Chloe said.

Kevin went to help her, wanting to make sure that she was all right.

"I don't think it is," he said.

Above them, the energy that was gathered there was starting to crackle unstably, spurts of it flaring off in random directions. He wondered what effect Purest Ro's armor, energy staff, and other devices would have on a weapon that was already filled to bursting with energy, on the verge of firing. He wondered what would happen to it when the whole of the Hive ship was already covered in cracks and fissures, barely holding together. He thought of the spikes of golden power on the surface, and what might happen if they had shifted even a little.

As more flares of energy flamed out, he decided that answer to that couldn't be good.

"We need to get out of here," Kevin said. "I think… I think it's going to explode."

"*How* do we get out of here?" Chloe asked, a sweep of her arm taking in the rest of the ship.

She had a point. By now, the place was almost deserted, ship after ship leaving through every opening it possessed. The big city ships were gone, the smaller ones filtering out wherever they could find the space. There might be more down there, but how long would it take to search a space the size of a small planet?

The weapon above them didn't look as though it would give them anywhere near enough time to find one and escape.

"We have to get off this ship," Kevin said again, looking around, trying to think of a way to do it. "Maybe the golden discs…"

Even as he said it, he knew it wouldn't work. The golden discs were connected to the Hive ship. They would only work within it. They might take him and Chloe as far as the aperture that looked out over the Earth, but the moment they passed that, they would fall away, leaving him and Chloe floating in space.

"The discs won't work," Chloe said, obviously having the same thought.

They needed to find something that would, and fast. Kevin could see the energy ball above them pulsing now, looking like a heart on the verge of bursting. He looked again at the aperture, and found himself thinking of all the things the Ilari had said about their suits… about their shields, and about how they would slow their fall if they came off their skidders. It wouldn't be enough, would it? It *couldn't* be enough.

What other option did they have?

"Chloe, do you trust me?" Kevin asked.

"Of course. Why?"

"I think… I think we need to jump."

"Jump?" Chloe asked.

Kevin explained his plan, and he could see the look of horror on Chloe's face while he did it.

"No, we can't, we'll be killed."

"We'll be killed if we stay here," Kevin pointed out. "We *have* to."

Chloe stood there thinking about it for heartbeat after heartbeat of the great ball of energy.

"Chloe…" Kevin said.

Chloe nodded. "All right, let's do this. Get on a disc."

Kevin stepped back onto the disc they'd taken, and felt it rise up underneath him, lifting them both from the platform. They rose through the Hive's world ship, heading for the aperture that looked out toward the Earth. They got closer and closer, rotating as they did so that now it sat below them like an image in a pool of water.

Kevin looked down at it, then over at Chloe.

"Ready?" he asked. Behind them, the energy ball was expanding again, this time beyond the borders of the platform, melting it as if it wasn't even there.

"I guess we'd better be," Chloe said.

Together they stepped up toward the edge of the platform, poised there like divers on the edge of a board. Kevin took the deepest breath he could…

…and leapt.

CHAPTER TWENTY

For the first few moments after they jumped, Kevin and Chloe fell so slowly that they might have been drifting. Kevin could feel himself moving along, completely weightless, the absence of pressure around him feeling completely open and empty. The force of their dive was enough to drag them away from the world ship's lack of external atmosphere, but now they were drifting along, the world ship growing smaller only slowly.

He could feel his lungs burning with the effort of his held breath, but he didn't dare to breathe, not trusting that there would be any oxygen there to pull in. Beside him, he could see Chloe doing the same, her face red against the otherwise monochrome background of space.

Eventually, he couldn't hold his breath anymore, and the gasp of escaping air briefly misted up the interior surface of the shield around his suit. He took another inward breath, and there was air there, either trapped by the same shield or manufactured by the suit. Kevin saw Chloe gasp for air a few seconds later, looking just as puzzled as he felt.

They kept falling, and now Kevin could feel the pull of the Earth below. They were close enough to it that its gravity dragged them in, snatching them from the grasp of the world ship, so that now they started to fall faster and faster, shooting down toward the planet below. From up here, Kevin could make out the landmasses and the vast expanses of ocean, the clouds and the weather systems moving across the surface.

Kevin heard Chloe's voice in his ear then, obviously carried by their suits. "It's so beautiful from up here," she said. "It all looks so *peaceful.*"

It did, Kevin had to admit. From this high, it wasn't possible to see the conflict that had ravaged the Earth, or the divisions that had driven home. He could still see some of the Ilari and Hive ships, but they weren't locked in conflict now. Instead, they hung there in space as if trying to make sense of everything that was happening around them, or maybe waiting to see what would happen next.

Even the waves of Hive ships fleeing the world ship were not greeted with energy fire now; the Ilari seemed to understand that these were not creatures controlled by the Hive, but free beings seeking to flee from the control of superiors who had forced them to ravage the universe. Their ships spread out, some fleeing deeper into space, some joining with the city ships, some making their way down toward the Earth faster than either Kevin or Chloe could.

They were going pretty fast by now though.

"Are you sure about our suits protecting us?" Chloe asked. Kevin could hear how frightened she sounded. "The AIs have this, right?"

"I'm sure it will be—" Kevin began, but a voice from his suit interrupted, obviously called up by the talk of AIs.

"Probability of a safe landing estimated at fifty percent," the AI's voice said, in a flat tone.

"Fifty percent?" Chloe shouted. "That's—"

"Chances of atmospheric burnup an additional ten percent. Chances of damage from flying debris—"

"Kevin, we're going to die!" Chloe yelled, although she didn't sound as though she was panicking. "We need to do something."

When had Chloe become someone who didn't panic anymore? Who just got on with trying to find a solution to things? Kevin didn't know, but he was glad that it had happened, for both of them. The only problem was that he couldn't see a way of doing anything right then that would help to make things better.

"At least we're off the world ship," he said, looking back. That was looking more fractured and dangerous by the second, energy pouring out of every crack and port on its surface so that it seemed to crackle with it. The fissures widened even as Kevin watched, sending tendrils of the expanding energy within reaching out into the space beyond.

Then the world ship exploded, and that energy burst out like the juice of an overripe fruit. Kevin saw rock and power and metal scatter in every direction, whole sections of the world ship breaking off like giant asteroids, flying out in the direction of deep space. One came closer to the world, and he saw Ilari ships rake it with energy blasts until it broke into smaller pieces, each burning up with a flare as it hit the atmosphere.

Kevin swallowed at the reminder of what might happen to him and Chloe in a moment.

The blast wave from the exploding ship hit them then, and the fact that it took so many seconds told Kevin how far they had already started to fall. The power of it pushed them forward, buffeting Kevin the way a storm might have slammed into the sails of a ship. It sent him spinning, corkscrewing down toward the world in a way that felt more like tumbling than flying.

They tumbled into the atmosphere, and it *hurt*.

Heat built up around Kevin and Chloe, so that Kevin could see it flaring on the surface of the suit's shields. They glowed yellow, then orange, then white hot. Most of the heat flared off, so that he and Chloe looked like comets shooting across the sky.

"Ow! That's *hot*!" Chloe said.

It was. The shields succeeded in flaring off most of the heat, but some of it was getting through. Kevin could feel himself getting hotter, so that at first he was uncomfortable, and then it was unpleasant, and then it just hurt.

Kevin cried out as he fell, and he could hear Chloe doing the same. The fall was too steep, too hard, the atmosphere feeling like sandpaper against his skin even though it was only air.

"Pull your arms in," Chloe yelled above the roar of the air around them. "Kevin, we have to pull our arms in."

Kevin understood what she meant: they had to try to make it so that they would cut through the air better, reducing the amount of them exposed to it. Pulling in his arms would turn him into a dart flying through the air, rather than a rasp juddering on top of it.

Even knowing that he needed to do it, actually managing it was still difficult. It felt as though his arms weighed more than lead, impossible to move, every inch of it a fight. But Kevin *did* fight, because the alternative seemed to be so much worse. The heat around him was unbearable, feeling as though an entire layer of his skin was being peeled off. If he hadn't spent so much of the last few months in pain, he never would have been able to bear it.

Little by little, he dragged his arms back to his side, trying to use the angle of his feet to steer, trying to turn himself into something that could fly down to the world, rather than something tumbling down to be destroyed. He could see the shields ahead of him thickening, obviously able to angle better now that he was one constant shape.

The heat wasn't a problem, but now it seemed that air was. Kevin guessed that there was only so much that the suit could do at once, and with whatever effort keeping them from burning up was taking, there didn't seem to be anything left over for oxygen. He gasped for air, feeling the lack of it pressing in around him and seeing shadows start to creep in on the edges of his vision.

Those grew, and Kevin knew that it would only be another few seconds before he passed out. Once he did that, he knew that he would go back to tumbling wildly, and that would be the end for him.

Then he broke down through the upper atmosphere, down into air that was at least breathable, despite being so thin that Kevin had to take great gulps of it just to keep from passing out. The sense of heat around him was passing as he and Chloe went down into layers of air that were thin, and cold, and almost enough to freeze them both as they fell.

"Spread out!" Kevin said, spreading his arms the way a skydiver might have to slow their freefall. "We need to go slower!"

He spread his arms out, seeing Chloe do the same opposite him. The two of them hung there in the sky, while Kevin could feel his suit pushing up, working to slow him even more. He could see water droplets and ice crystals on a shield above him, spread out like a parachute, or perhaps the wings of some great creature.

It gave him plenty of time to look down at the world below. From this high, Kevin could see land and water, the world spread out beneath him almost like a map.

"We need to pick where we're going," Kevin said.

"*Can* we pick?" Chloe asked.

Kevin twisted slightly in the air as an answer, and felt himself move forward with Chloe alongside him. It seemed that the suits' shields meant that they could glide through the air as well as just falling slower than they had any right to.

Even so, Kevin was pretty sure that they would need something else. What had the AI said? Fifty-fifty odds of a safe landing weren't enough.

"Water," he said. "If we head for water, at least we won't hit anything when we land."

"It's better than running into a mountain," Chloe agreed.

Kevin looked out for the point where the land and the water met, aiming for a space dotted with small islands. He didn't know where it was, or even what part of the world they were presently flying over.

They were getting lower now, still moving far faster than Kevin thought they should be. He could feel the shield above them pulling them upward, slowing them down gently, holding them hanging in the sky.

They were still over land, and now Kevin wasn't sure if they were going to make it to the spot where the water lapped up against the shore. If they didn't... well, there were a lot of jagged rocks down there, and if all the shields from their suits were busy trying to slow them, he doubted they would do much to keep Kevin and Chloe from being punctured by them.

He pushed forward, straining as if doing so might keep them from slamming into the ground. They kept moving, so low that Kevin felt his leg brush a tree as they passed, and now they plunged off the edge of a cliff, the water below them.

They skimmed along for another few tens of seconds, and now Kevin could see the shields around him and Chloe reshaping themselves again. The sea was there below them, getting closer by the moment until they finally hit it with a splash that seemed to fill the world. Kevin felt himself plunging down into the water, and saw Chloe dropping almost as quickly. Worse, she seemed to be dropping through the water limply, no sign that she was trying to fight against it. Had the impact knocked her out?

Kevin swam for her, managing to hook an arm around her, and then swimming for the surface with all the strength he had. The light of it seemed to be a long way away now, every stroke taking forever, while all the time Kevin found himself wondering what else might be in the water with them.

They broke through the surface of the water, and now Chloe spluttered, spitting out water as she came back to herself.

"Are you okay?" Kevin asked her.

It took her a moment before she nodded. "I'm fine. I... did we really just do that?"

"We did," Kevin said. He looked around. "Where are we?"

There was no obvious answer to that. A little way off, Kevin could see an island, palm trees sticking out from a small space of sand and greenery. Kevin pointed to it and saw Chloe nod, then together the two started to swim for it.

It was such a long way that Kevin wasn't sure that either of them would make it. The current fought them with every stroke, and by now, Kevin could feel the effects of everything that they had just been through. His body felt raw, as if it had been stripped clean by falling through the atmosphere, while bruises felt as though they covered every inch of him.

The two of them kept swimming anyway, and now Kevin could feel waves pushing the two of them in toward a beach. After what seemed like an eternity, he felt sand under his feet, and managed to shift from swimming to walking, or at least staggering.

The two of them stumbled up onto the beach, and Kevin collapsed down onto his knees. Beside him, Chloe fell down onto her back, staring up, and Kevin decided that he didn't have the energy to do more than that either. He fell down onto his back in the sand, feeling it in his hair while they both looked up at the sky.

Above them, pieces of the world ship were still burning up in the atmosphere, leaving streaks and lines of fire. Somehow, that hadn't been them. Somehow, almost impossibly, they'd survived it, and done more than that.

"We did it," Kevin said. "We actually beat the Hive."

"Don't say it," Chloe replied. "It feels as though every time we say something like that, something worse comes along. I'm not sure I can handle something worse."

Kevin had to admit that Chloe had a point. Right now, it felt like even standing would be a challenge, let alone some new kind of enemy. Instead of saying anything, he just lay there, looking up, watching the fireworks display that marked the end of the Hive's world ship.

"How long do we wait?" Kevin asked after a while.

"What?"

"How long do we wait for the next bad thing to show up?" Kevin asked. "I mean, do we just lie here and wait for it, or do we get up?"

That was enough to make Chloe laugh, and soon, Kevin felt himself joining in that laughter. They'd done it. They'd actually done it. This was over.

Slowly, Kevin managed to get himself back to his feet, and Chloe did the same beside him. He looked around the island they were on, seeing rocks and sand, trees and grass. It was the kind of place that might have seemed like a paradise if they hadn't just landed there out of nowhere.

"We're stuck here, aren't we?" Chloe said.

Kevin had been trying not to think that, but the more he thought about it, the more he realized that she was right. They were on an island, with no idea where they were, no people there to help them, and no sign of anything else.

Would they be stuck there like that forever? The island didn't seem so bad, with all the resources someone might need to survive. It probably wouldn't be such a bad place, but just the thought of being stuck there with no choice made Kevin look out wistfully toward the horizon.

"We need to find shelter," he said.

Chloe nodded beside him. "Shelter, and water, and food, and fire."

Maybe a month ago, it would all have sounded too daunting, but by now, they had both survived everything the world could throw at them. Everything at least three worlds could throw, in fact.

They set off onto the island, and Kevin tried to work out if any of the rocks there would be sharp enough to use as a tool.

They worked together, starting to gather branches and leaves. The sound of running water promised a stream or a spring, while Kevin was pretty sure that he could hear the rustling of small animals in the undergrowth. They would find a way to survive this, for as long as it took, even if that proved to be forever.

He hoped that it wouldn't be. Luna was back in LA, and Kevin couldn't imagine the thought of having been through all of this if he couldn't get back to her afterward.

As it started to get dark, they built a fire out on the shore, clicking flinty stones together until they produced sparks to fall down onto a small ball of leaves and twigs. Kevin sat with his back to the trees, looking out over the water.

That was why he saw the Ilari ship skimming in over the horizon before Chloe did.

It was sleek and dart-like, a little bigger than one of the Hive's smaller ships, and obviously something transported by one of the bigger Ilari craft sitting up above the world. It moved quickly, and so low that furrows ran along the wave tops where its engines pressed against it.

The ship skidded in close, circling the island, and Kevin grabbed a branch from the fire to wave it. Chloe did the same, and soon they were standing on the beach, doing everything they could to attract attention.

The Ilari ship came in close, settling down onto the surface of the water as if it were a more normal kind of ship. A hatch opened, light spilling from it, and in that light, Kevin saw the one set of features that he had longed to see more than any others.

"Did you two want a ride?" Luna asked.

CHAPTER TWENTY ONE

"We followed tracking signals on your suits," Luna said, with a gesture toward General s'Lara. "The general said that—"

Right then, Kevin didn't care what the general had said, only that Luna was there, in front of him, and she was safe, and they had won this. He threw his arms around her, crushing her close.

"I missed you," he said, because it was the only thing that he could think of to say.

"I missed you too," Luna said. Her hand held onto the back of his head, her fingers caught up in Kevin's hair so that he could feel their tips against his scalp. This close, he could feel as if they were one person, not two. "From the moment you went up into the world ship, I thought—"

"I know," Kevin said, because he'd thought it too. When he'd gone there, he hadn't expected to come back. He hadn't even dared to hope, not really.

"And then when it blew up…" Luna went on. Kevin was surprised to hear her sounding that frightened about it, that vulnerable. Normally, Luna was too tough to ever let herself sound vulnerable.

"I know," Kevin said, more softly this time. He pulled back from Luna just enough that he could look into her eyes. Even that felt like too much space, and he wanted to close the gap between them then and kiss her. Two things stopped him: one was that they were in a ship that also contained Chloe and General s'Lara, along with a pair of other Ilari who were obviously there in case of trouble.

The other was that Bobby chose that moment to jump up at them, knocking them both off balance and causing them to laugh.

"Yes, yes, I missed you too," Kevin said. He stepped back and ruffled the dog's fur.

He saw Luna turn to Chloe. "Thank you for bringing him back."

"What are friends for?" Chloe replied, and the two girls actually seemed happy around one another, with no hint of the rivalry or jibes that had been there for so much of their time together.

Luna actually hugged Chloe then, and that seemed to catch her almost as off balance as it did Kevin.

"I'm glad you're safe too," Luna said.

"You were the one stuck in the middle of a battle when we left," Chloe pointed out. "Besides, the most difficult part of it all was making sure that Kevin didn't mess up the plan."

"Hey!" Kevin protested, but he seemed to be outnumbered for the moment.

General s'Lara stood up from the pilot's seat, coming back toward them while another of the Ilari took over. She held Kevin out at arm's length, looking into his eyes as if searching, and Kevin knew exactly what she would be searching for.

"I'm not controlled by the Hive again," he promised.

"You can't be too careful," the general replied. "All of this seems almost too good to be true, so there's still a part of me that wants to make sure it isn't a trick."

Kevin could understand that; even he was having a little trouble believing that all of this had really happened the way he thought it had, and he'd been there for it. He'd felt the pressure of the world ship blowing up. He'd seen Purest Lux fall into the energy weapon and destabilize it.

"What do your sensors tell you?" Kevin asked. "What does your AI say?"

"I don't even need it for the obvious one," General s'Lara said. "Because my *eyes* say that their world ship is destroyed. As for the rest of it... it seems to be over."

Over was good. Kevin wished that they could just leave it at over. Even so, he needed to know all of it.

"What exactly has happened?" he asked.

"You first," Luna said from the side. "I want to hear all about how you saved the world."

Kevin could hear the yearning there, and he couldn't work out if it was the same yearning that he felt toward her, or simply that she'd wished she could have been there for the last part of it, or both.

"You couldn't go," Chloe said. "They called it Luna's Army. It wouldn't have worked if you weren't there. You were too important."

"You're important too," Luna assured her, putting a hand on her arm. Was it a coincidence, Kevin wondered, that she picked the arm that the Hive had bonded with one of their living devices?

"Tell us what happened on the world ship," General s'Lara prompted. "I need to understand what happened there."

Kevin explained as best he could. He told her about the signal, and the disruption it had caused, about the aliens fleeing their ship once the Hive didn't control them, and about the final race to try to stop Purest Lux from destroying the Earth. Finally, he told them about the way he and Chloe had escaped just ahead of the blast.

"It must have overridden many of the safety measures to try to fire the device before it was ready," General s'Lara said. "That would explain why it was so unstable."

"Really?" Luna said. "These two skydive, or space-dive, or whatever down to Earth, and *that's* the part you're focusing on?"

"I'll admit, that is rather impressive," General s'Lara said. "I must try it sometime…" She looked away in the way she did when her AI was talking to her, and Kevin had a brief glimpse of projections and simulations. "Or not. You two realize that you were *incredibly* lucky to survive?"

"But we did," Chloe said, "and that's the part that matters. Besides, it was *so* cool."

Kevin saw the general smile at that, though it was obvious that she was trying to look stern.

"Cool, yes." General s'Lara appeared to consider for a minute. "I'm glad to hear the way things were up there. Even though the Hive were our enemies, I wouldn't like to think of all the creatures they controlled being trapped aboard their world ship when it was destroyed."

"We saw their ships pouring out and we thought it might be another attack," Luna said. "But at the same time, everyone we were fighting just… stopped."

"Stopped is the wrong word," the general pointed out. "They were not still, and some did not stop fighting. They were freed, and some were freed to be wild, or cruel, or so mad that they sought to kill everything."

Luna nodded, and there was something about the way she did it that said that things had been anything but easy, even in the moments after Kevin had channeled the Ilari's signals. But then, he'd seen it for himself; he'd seen the way the Hive's ship had fallen into fighting when its creatures were freed, because some of them knew nothing else except how to fight, and some of them had that much hatred of their former masters. A few were even loyal.

"So you won the battle?" Kevin asked. He wanted to be sure.

"Better," Luna said. "After whatever you did up there, there wasn't even a battle, not really. There were *some* creatures we had to fight, but all of the controlled people either stood there or came over to us, and most of the aliens did, or they ran, or they fought with each other. Even the ships flew off."

It sounded perfect. Well, no, actually it sounded chaotic and difficult and like it filled the world with whatever monsters the Hive had unleashed in it, but at least it meant that the fighting had stopped.

"There will be a lot to do, in time," General s'Lara said. "We will need to decide what to do with those creatures left on Earth. What do we do when they have no home? What do we do when they are nothing but things built in the flesh factories to kill?"

It seemed like a lot, but it also seemed like a bizarrely wonderful problem to have. It was the kind of problem that came only because they had won, *because* the Hive didn't have control over the creatures anymore.

"We'll work something out," Kevin said.

Chloe nodded, looking determined.

"General," the pilot said, "we are getting close. I will be taking us in to land in a moment."

"Thank you, Lanx. Take us down."

They landed, and Kevin could see the huge crowds of people standing around the quarry, looking as though they didn't know what to do next. Most were human, but many were not. He could see small Ilari ships coming and going, apparently transporting people here and there.

"We are taking the ones who want to go back to their lives back to the places they remember," General s'Lara said.

"And we're having the ones who are staying for now bury the dead," Luna added. A part of Kevin admired that she had been able to organize so much in such a short time; another part of him hated that she'd had to. They were both supposed to still be kids, after all.

When they went out of the shuttle, it was obvious just how much she was the heart of it all. Maybe him too. The crowd there stopped when they landed, human and alien, Ilari and Hive, all turning to stare at them. For a moment, the coordination of it all was enough that Kevin thought maybe they'd failed, and somehow the Hive had reasserted control over everything.

Then the first people started to applaud.

They clapped, and they stamped, whooped and yelled, the noise rippling out around the walls of the quarry before turning into a crescendo. It felt completely overwhelming to be at the heart of that, and in it, Kevin thought that he could hear people shouting his name, and Luna's and…

"Wait, that's my *mom's* voice!" he said.

Beside him, General s'Lara smiled.

"And that's *my* mom," Luna said, "and my dad, and… aren't those the people from the NASA institute?"

It was, and Kevin looked from them to General s'Lara and back, not knowing what to say.

"Our people are very good at finding people, it turns out," she said. "We thought that, after everything you've done, you should be the first ones reunited."

"Thank you," Kevin said, and he would have hugged the general except that in that moment there was only one person he wanted to hug. He pushed his way through the crowd of people, although the truth was that he didn't have to push much. People stepped back for him, apparently in awe. He could see Cub there, starting to step toward him and Luna, but Luna just pushed past him and Cub turned to head off in the other direction. Kevin might have asked her about that, but they both had something more important to do than any question they could ask. He made his way to his mother, threw his arms around her, and held tight while beside them Bobby barked excitedly.

"You're alive!" he said, holding onto her. "I'm so…"

There weren't words for what he was. His mother was alive, and not controlled, and safe. Happy wasn't enough for that. Glad would have been an insult to everything he felt.

"I love you so much," his mother said, and held him out at arms' length. "They tell me that you did all this; that you saved us."

"Not just me," Kevin insisted. He gestured over to where Luna was reuniting with her own parents, obviously just as happy as he was in that moment. "Luna did a lot of it, and Chloe…" A thought came to him, and for a second, doubts intruded on Kevin's happiness. "Mom, I have to go make sure that Chloe is okay."

"Then I'm coming with you," his mother said. "After all of this, I'm not letting you out of my sight again."

Kevin made his way back through the crowd to the spot where Chloe had been. He was surprised to find Luna moving on the same path. Obviously they'd had the same thought when it came to their friend.

General s'Lara was waiting for them, but there was no sign of Chloe right then.

"She is over that way," the general said, gesturing. "She is safe. I know enough to know not to bring *her* family anywhere near her. She will need a little time, though. In the meantime, there are people who need to talk to you two."

"Do they need to, or do they just *want* to?" Kevin's mother asked.

General s'Lara paused for a moment. "There is a man claiming to be the President of this place. Is he the President of Earth, or something else?"

"The President wants to speak to us?" Luna asked.

"I think that there are many people who do. For one thing, you have what appears to be an army, and I imagine people will want to know what you want to do with it. There will be people who want to talk about rebuilding, and about what happens next, and—"

"And I'm sure Kevin and Luna will be happy to talk to them soon," Kevin's mother said. "But not now. Now, they're going to see their friend. They've earned that much, at least."

Kevin couldn't have been more grateful for his mother being there than he was in that moment. He, Luna, and Bobby set off through the crowd again, and he thought that he caught a glimpse of Professor Brewster beckoning to him, but he also saw the former soldier, Ted, pulling the scientist back. Apparently, at least some things didn't change.

"Eventually, they will want us to deal with complicated things," Luna said.

"Not now though," Kevin said.

"Not now," Luna agreed.

They went to the spot where Chloe was sitting on a flat piece of rock. Bobby went alongside her, hugging close to her. Luna and Kevin did the same.

"We're sorry," Luna said, putting an arm around her.

"For going to your families?" Chloe said. "For having families happy enough that you want to? You shouldn't apologize for that. It's not your fault that I have—"

"Don't say 'nothing,'" Kevin said. "You have us."

"Yes," Chloe said with a smile, "I do, and it's really wonderful, you know? But eventually, the world is going to start to settle down. All the adults are going to start running things again, and I'll be a girl left on her own, or in a home, or—"

"You could stay with one of us," Luna said, and it meant a lot to Kevin that she was the one making that offer. It obviously meant a lot to Chloe too, because Kevin could see the tears in her eyes.

"Thank you, both of you. You're… you're the best friends I've ever had. General s'Lara already made me a different offer, though."

"What kind of offer?" Kevin asked.

Chloe gestured to where people and aliens were still milling around, trying to make sense of things. "Look at this. The whole world is changed now. Whole galaxies have changed, and people will need to make sense of it. There are creatures on Earth that are dangerous, even without the Hive to push them into being horrors. There are whole other fragments of the Hive out there somewhere. There are worlds that need to be rebuilt, and fights out there, and a whole universe full of things I haven't seen…"

"You're going with them, aren't you?" Kevin guessed.

Chloe nodded. "I think so. I never really fit in on Earth, so why not? And the Hive made me strong and fast, they gave me this arm…" She held up her altered arm. "No one even knows what I can do. Maybe the Ilari can help me find out."

"I…" Kevin hugged her hard. Luna did the same, until they were all hugging together. "I'll miss you so much."

"So will I," Luna agreed. "And I'll be really jealous of you too."

"I think I'm the one who gets to be jealous," Chloe said with a look between Luna and Kevin. "No, it's okay. I'm happy for you, both of you. Be happy for me too?"

"We are," Kevin assured her. He guessed that there weren't many happy endings for Chloe on Earth. Maybe up in space, she could find everything she'd ever hoped for.

Chloe stood, walking off in the direction of General s'Lara. That left Kevin and Luna sitting on the rock, with Bobby at their feet.

"We're going to have to work out so many things," Kevin said.

"Like who gets Bobby?" Luna said. "Simple, I do. That way, you have to visit me lots."

"I think they're going to want us to work out more than that," Kevin said, with a glance back toward where an assortment of official-looking people were starting to gather around General s'Lara.

"I figure they'll want to know what we're supposed to do about food, and water, and government, and about a million different things," Luna said. Kevin put a hand on her cheek, smoothing away the frown that was starting to grow there.

"Maybe if we leave them long enough they'll realize that *they're* the adults here, and maybe they should be working this stuff out," Kevin suggested.

"What, deal with all of it and leave us both to go back to being ordinary kids?" Luna asked.

Kevin smiled at that, because he didn't think either of them would ever be that ordinary. "Maybe."

"Is that what you want? You want to go home? You want it all to be normal?" Luna asked.

Kevin barely had to think about it before he nodded. It had been pretty much all that he had wanted since the doctors first told him he was dying, and now that he wasn't, well, it seemed like as much of an adventure as any battle could be.

"Yes," he said. "I want a normal life for a while where we both just get to be kids. Well, as long as you're there."

"That sounds good to me," Luna said. She put her arms around his shoulders. "Particularly the part with you."

Kevin couldn't tell which of them kissed the other first in that moment. He wasn't sure it mattered.

All that mattered was that they were there together, and they had won, and everything else…

Everything else could wait awhile.

NOW AVAILABLE!

A NEW SERIES!

THE MAGIC FACTORY
(Oliver Blue and the School for Seers—Book One)

"A powerful opener to a series [that] will produce a combination of feisty protagonists and challenging circumstances to thoroughly involve not just young adults, but adult fantasy fans who seek epic stories fueled by powerful friendships and adversaries."
--Midwest Book Review (Diane Donovan) (re *A Throne for Sisters*)

"Morgan Rice's imagination is limitless!"
--Books and Movie Reviews (re *A Throne for Sisters*)

From #1 Bestselling fantasy author Morgan Rice comes a new series for middle grade readers—and adults, too! Fans of Harry Potter and Percy Jackson—look no further!

THE MAGIC FACTORY: OLIVER BLUE AND THE SCHOOL FOR SEERS (BOOK ONE) tells the story of 11 year old Oliver Blue, a boy unloved by his hateful family. Oliver knows he is different, and senses that he holds powers that others do not. Obsessed with inventions, Oliver is determined to escape his horrible life and make his mark on the world.

When Oliver is moved to yet another awful house he is put into in a new sixth grade, one even more terrifying than the last. He is bullied and excluded, and sees no way out. But when he stumbles across an abandoned invention factory, he wonders if his dreams might be about to come true.

Who is the mysterious old inventor hiding in the factory?

What is his secret invention?

And will Oliver end up transported back in time, to 1944, to a magical school for kids with powers to rival his own?

An uplifting fantasy, THE MAGIC FACTORY is book #1 in a riveting new series filled with magic, love, humor, heartbreak, tragedy, destiny, and a series of shocking twists. It will make you fall in love with Oliver Blue, and keep you turning pages late into the night.

Book #2 in the series (THE ORB OF KANDRA) and Book #3 (THE OBSIDIANS) are now also available!

"The beginnings of something remarkable are there."
--San Francisco Book Review (re *A Quest of Heroes*)

Books by Morgan Rice

OLIVER BLUE AND THE SCHOOL FOR SEERS
THE MAGIC FACTORY (Book #1)
THE ORB OF KANDRA (Book #2)
THE OBSIDIANS (Book #3)
THE SCEPTOR OF FIRE (Book #4)

THE INVASION CHRONICLES
TRANSMISSION (Book #1)
ARRIVAL (Book #2)
ASCENT (Book #3)
RETURN (Book #4)

THE WAY OF STEEL
ONLY THE WORTHY (Book #1)

A THRONE FOR SISTERS
A THRONE FOR SISTERS (Book #1)
A COURT FOR THIEVES (Book #2)
A SONG FOR ORPHANS (Book #3)
A DIRGE FOR PRINCES (Book #4)
A JEWEL FOR ROYALS (BOOK #5)
A KISS FOR QUEENS (BOOK #6)
A CROWN FOR ASSASSINS (Book #7)
A CLASP FOR HEIRS (Book #8)

OF CROWNS AND GLORY
SLAVE, WARRIOR, QUEEN (Book #1)
ROGUE, PRISONER, PRINCESS (Book #2)
KNIGHT, HEIR, PRINCE (Book #3)
REBEL, PAWN, KING (Book #4)
SOLDIER, BROTHER, SORCERER (Book #5)
HERO, TRAITOR, DAUGHTER (Book #6)
RULER, RIVAL, EXILE (Book #7)
VICTOR, VANQUISHED, SON (Book #8)

KINGS AND SORCERERS
RISE OF THE DRAGONS (Book #1)
RISE OF THE VALIANT (Book #2)
THE WEIGHT OF HONOR (Book #3)

A FORGE OF VALOR (Book #4)
A REALM OF SHADOWS (Book #5)
NIGHT OF THE BOLD (Book #6)

THE SORCERER'S RING
A QUEST OF HEROES (Book #1)
A MARCH OF KINGS (Book #2)
A FATE OF DRAGONS (Book #3)
A CRY OF HONOR (Book #4)
A VOW OF GLORY (Book #5)
A CHARGE OF VALOR (Book #6)
A RITE OF SWORDS (Book #7)
A GRANT OF ARMS (Book #8)
A SKY OF SPELLS (Book #9)
A SEA OF SHIELDS (Book #10)
A REIGN OF STEEL (Book #11)
A LAND OF FIRE (Book #12)
A RULE OF QUEENS (Book #13)
AN OATH OF BROTHERS (Book #14)
A DREAM OF MORTALS (Book #15)
A JOUST OF KNIGHTS (Book #16)
THE GIFT OF BATTLE (Book #17)

THE SURVIVAL TRILOGY
ARENA ONE: SLAVERSUNNERS (Book #1)
ARENA TWO (Book #2)
ARENA THREE (Book #3)

VAMPIRE, FALLEN
BEFORE DAWN (Book #1)

THE VAMPIRE JOURNALS
TURNED (Book #1)
LOVED (Book #2)
BETRAYED (Book #3)
DESTINED (Book #4)
DESIRED (Book #5)
BETROTHED (Book #6)
VOWED (Book #7)
FOUND (Book #8)
RESURRECTED (Book #9)
CRAVED (Book #10)

FATED (Book #11)
OBSESSED (Book #12)

About Morgan Rice

Morgan Rice is the #1 bestselling and USA Today bestselling author of the epic fantasy series THE SORCERER'S RING, comprising seventeen books; of the #1 bestselling series THE VAMPIRE JOURNALS, comprising twelve books; of the #1 bestselling series THE SURVIVAL TRILOGY, a post-apocalyptic thriller comprising three books; of the epic fantasy series KINGS AND SORCERERS, comprising six books; of the epic fantasy series OF CROWNS AND GLORY, comprising eight books; of the epic fantasy series A THRONE FOR SISTERS, comprising eight books; of the new science fiction series THE INVASION CHRONICLES, comprising four books; and of the new fantasy series OLIVER BLUE AND THE SCHOOL FOR SEERS, comprising three books (and counting). Morgan's books are available in audio and print editions, and translations are available in over 25 languages.

Morgan loves to hear from you, so please feel free to visit www.morganricebooks.com to join the email list, receive a free book, receive free giveaways, download the free app, get the latest exclusive news, connect on Facebook and Twitter, and stay in touch!

www.ingramcontent.com/pod-product-compliance
Lightning Source LLC
Chambersburg PA
CBHW070551100726
47907CB00004B/1337